THE INTERSECTION

Marshall May

Creationatorium LLC

To all of my friends since school
Each of you has helped me write this is your own way

To my family
For showing me unconditional love
I didn't know how rare it was

To Sarah
You have made all of this possible
I will love you forever and a day

CONTENTS

Title Page

Copyright

Dedication

~Monday~   1

Luminescence   3

Soft Labor   7

Waste   14

Habit   21

Harsh Sincerity   28

Search for Wisdom   33

Withered Lament   38

~Monday Night~   43

Dare to Wander   44

Nostalgia   54

A Welcome Neighbor   59

Disclosure   66

~Tuesday~   71

Sunrise   72

Hard Decisions   77

Welcome Healing   85

~Friday~   91

Drowning Nectar   92

Lost Divinity   99

~Saturday~   107

Lamenting Heaven   108

An Honest Narrator   113

Lingering Need   119

~Sunday~   127

A Sage Nudge   128

Secret Dread   135

~MONDAY~

LUMINESCENCE

Chapter 1

Dust floats in the air, swirling across beams of colored light. Cascades of cerulean and scarlet emanate from stained glass. High walls encircle the images made of glass with intricate stone carvings detailed by master craftsmen.

The hard wooden pews crafted with reverence. Rough edges clash against the soft flow of the grain lines. Plush crimson kneelers with the telltale fade of use. Candle holders line the walls with the wax drippings of a thousand candles. And the altar. Clad in red and gold. At the end of a hundred pews with one hundred times the rough edges and soft lines, with one hundred times the kneelers. At the forefront lies the sacred line. The boundary between the ordinary and the hallowed, where a cracker transforms into flesh and wine into blood, where a man dons a robe to become the voice of the divine.

Softly spoken words create a gentle hum that flows out from the wooden pews. Such soft reverence for this holy place. His words are meant for no one's ears but his own, and, for he who can hear through any man's ears.

He... is a simple man. Short blonde hair, a white dress shirt wrinkled from lack of care. Dress slacks obviously bought from the cheapest store he could find. Black shoes with scuff marks from never being shined a day in their life. A simple man that leads a simple life; if someone looked into his wallet and found more than one credit card, an ID, and $12 to his name, most would be absolutely shocked.

And here he sits. Not for the world to see, not even for God to see, but for a sense of purpose. To pray for the need to pray. Praying for the life he wanted when he was 12, sitting in pews just like these with his mom on Sundays. These 15 years have done very little to the dream he held so dear. Faith that a simple life in service to the Lord would make him a better man.

Slowly, a difference starts to form. It's not something you could see or hear or notice in any meaningful way. But, for this man, for Luke, the changes to his life have the possibility to upheave everything he's held dear.

Luke becomes quiet. Eyes closed, palms together. A final prayer that is more than any word or set of words could give justice. It's closest to a plea, for safety and peace in the time to come. An admission of God's presence without the want or need of something in return. As Luke finishes his final ritual in this holy place, he smiles. Opening his eyes, as the smile fades.

The pleasure he felt taking part in his final ritual was slipping. Upon standing, the feeling will have dissipated from all but his memory.

Luke realizes he doesn't know how long he's been motionless. Slight redness forms in his cheeks as he looks around the church to see if anyone else was there to notice. Seeing no one, Luke walks to the main door, red fading with every step.

Opening the front door casts the warmth of light from a mid-day sun, warming the left side of Luke's face and neck. Stopping for only a half step to take in a deep breath; to feel the warmth of the sun. Noise! The almost ever present bustle of those around him is coming back. Luke's ears try to keep the onslaught of sounds at bay for as long as they can. But, the City that lives around him would not be stopped, or turned down for long.

Down the steps and a quick right turn. Luke was now one of many. All walking down the street with a singular purpose. To be somewhere, anywhere, anywhere but where they currently stood. The familiar sights of markets and shops pass from view and back into memory.

Rays of light heat Luke's back to a warm haze, melting the aches of muscles. Luke slips into a slight slowing in pace as the warmth causes his mind to go blank. Jogged out of his stupor by the flow of others on the street passing him by, Luke returns to the flow. He thinks of those surrounding him on the sidewalk. Do they feel the same warmth on their backs? And does it seem to warm their souls as deeply as it does his?

Luke looks at his watch.

"Oh, no... I'm going to get called out again."

He picks up the pace. Sliding by those walking the street slower than him with the ease of someone that lived their entire life in the city.

An entire city at his disposal. Nights of dancing, corners with drugs, and restaurants full of people enjoying each other's company. Yet, Luke refuses himself these things and more. The church. Yes. The church is the one thing that gives Luke any sense of constancy. Every day before work he goes to light a candle, Sunday mass, evening mass five times a week, and lastly he gives up his lunch break for silent prayer.

Luke's problem is that he has been coming into work and back from lunch late more often than not in the past two weeks. It wasn't a problem at first because he had such an outstanding record of coming in on time. Others noticed when it became the standard and not the exception. His boss kept a close eye on his comings and goings.

Luke knows he should stop going to church during his lunch break. This has already cost him dearly and might even lead to him being fired if it keeps up. A part of him wishes to keep away, but the allure pulls him back every day. Faith has always played a large role in Luke's life, since he was a small child sitting in the pews next to his mother. Unfortunately, sermons and candles have had little value of late. Only independent prayer like the kind he can only do during lunch has been doing anything as of late. That feeling he's been chasing. A serene moment of fleeting clarity that gets Luke through the day, only to disappear faster than it grew.

A frown breaks across Luke's face.

What if the feeling from his lunchtime prayers diminishes? He's known this for a while, but only now has he been able to put his fears into words. Without realizing it, Luke has been chasing those last moments with God more and more. How long until something gives way?

Passing through a lobby with sleek armchairs ergonomically made to feel uncomfortable after 30 minutes of sitting. Heading for the elevators in the back cubby area behind the guards.

"No, no, No..." says Luke.

The clock above the elevators are showing him what he already knew but didn't want to admit. Luke is already 23 minutes late. With a wait for an elevator and the ride to his floor... Luke's extremely worried. He hopes no one realizes just how late he is.

A quick ride up an elevator and the doors slowly slide open. A small sigh of relief comes from Luke, as he doesn't see his boss anywhere in sight. He steps off the elevator and begins walking to his cubicle.

This, is when Seth takes notice.

SOFT LABOR

Chapter 2

Seth is the youngest Branch Manager in the company's history. He didn't get there by being nice. That being said, he didn't get there by being mean either. He got to be a branch manager through hard work, luck, and knowing what questions to ask. Most of the people he manages, his friends, or his colleagues don't understand his mindset about asking questions. To Seth, asking a question means knowing your limitations and the limitations of those you're asking. One question can mean the difference between costing the company $150,000 or being the hero that saved it.

Seth is currently watching the room. It's something he loves to do whenever he has the time. Because of Seth's height, he can see all the way to the other end of the building. This allows him to see which people move around, who never seem to move, or those that can't seem to stay still even when in their cubicle. Watching the movements of his employees was like asking them questions about themselves they can't help but answer. Do you drink 5 cups of coffee a day? How long do you talk with the person in the cubicle next to you?

"Did you come back from lunch late?" asks Seth under his breath.

Navigating the twists and turns of the cubicle maze; Luke

is gradually making the way to his workstation. Past the men huddled near the water cooler in the third row and around to the middle row. Sliding through the group of people just walking and talking trying to disguise their lack of working. Debrah from the mailroom comes around a corner and hands Luke a bundle of mail before continuing down the alley. While looking through his mail, Luke makes the final few turns into his cubicle. As he logs back into his computer, the man one cubicle over pops his head up and leans over the divider.

"Hey... Seth came by a little earlier when you were gone. Sooo be careful."

Luke hangs his head a little. "Thanks Bill, I appreciate the help."

"Gotta stick together right. Keep the big man off each other's backs."

Lifting his head to smile and with a small laughing nod, "Thanks again."

After Bill sits back down to work, Seth walks back into his office and nearly collapses in front of his computer. Logging into the company management system, he looks up the login/ logout schedule for Luke's computer. A blip... Flashes of lines dart across the monitor as the screen freezes for a few seconds. This has been happening recently; the system seems to be slowly deteriorating. Problem was, the good-for-nothings in the IT department haven't been able to solve the problem. Tapping and hastily moving the mouse back and forth for a few seconds, then the blips happen again and the screen returns the cursor to movement. Seth shrugs it off for now and continues his investigation. The screen confirmed the truth of what Seth expected.

"What... is... the question?"

Luke looks over his shoulder again. This is the tenth time in as many minutes. Keeping his eyes on the screen is getting harder to do. Maybe a quick look at the corner office will help ease the paranoia of being crept up on. Lifting out of the chair and just high enough to have a line of sight over the cubicle wall shows no sign of anyone even looking in his direction. Panning his gaze through a full 360 shows no one looking directly at him. Paranoia seems to fade, and he can feel a smile slowly spreading on his face. A slight collapse into his chair causes the delusions of Seth to subside. He thinks about how stupid, how foolish he is worrying about Seth coming over and firing him. So Luke resumes his work. But, there is something. Something nagging Luke in the back of his mind.

Why would he fire me?

Why indeed? It's true that he hasn't been coming in on time, but everyone has periods of time when that happens. Even taking too long at lunch pales in comparison to how little some people in the office seem to work. And he wouldn't need to worry about his own job until Seth fires them. Right? Except, he HAS been clearing out the non-workers. Even the ones that try to buddy up to him to be more important in the eyes of the boss are let go if they don't work harder after Seth gives them a few warnings. Similar to the warnings that Seth had given about coming in late from lunch just two days ago.

Oh no, what if he was just waiting to get permission from HR?

And so, for the eleventh time in just as many minutes... Luke is looking over his shoulder and popping his head above the cubicle wall to see towards Seth's office.

Seth takes his time, looking at the computer screen with a security cameras' view of Luke's cubicle. Counting the times he sees Luke looking over the edge towards this very office. He started laughing after the fourth time, as an ever wider smile grew on his face. After a particularly wide smile, another employee catches Luke looking around, and he quickly retreats into his cubicle. Seth makes his move.

Calmly walking out of his office and making an immediate

turn to the left.

This was one of his minor pleasures, creeping up on unexpecting people. Especially when they were looking out for him, as it added a bit of a challenge to find the path that would keep him hidden long enough. Most people wouldn't have guessed this was something he enjoyed. Others believed this to be true with no actual evidence. They believed they were so engrossed in their work that they simply missed the sound of his shoes or the slight jingle in his pockets. If they paid just a little more attention, they would have noticed the fact that those sounds hadn't actually happened, leading up to the shock of Seth suddenly appearing.

Seth rounds the corner into the first corridor of cubicles.

He sometimes believes that he does this to keep his workers off guard. Not allowing them time to be scared and grasp at excuses. When he thought of it like that, wasn't he doing them a favor? Like ripping off a bandaid in one quick motion.

In reality, the reason he sneaks up on people was for the childish joy he feels. Such a feeling that comes from sneaking up on a person who didn't know they were about to be pounced upon. The rush of pleasure comes from someone's terror spreading and then quickly evaporating into relaxation.

Going around the corner into the row of cubicles where Luke worked.

Luke sees movement to his left. A gentle bobbing of hair above the wall of his cubicle. Glancing at the movement showed it was more of a glide than he originally thought, this puzzled Luke on an almost subconscious level. Typing speed slows, eyes widen, breathing hastens as the hair gliding towards the opening of the cubicle becomes more recognizable.

Seth rounds the last corner and sees a pale and surprised Luke.

Damn, he noticed me before the turn. "Luke, how are you?"

That was the question. 'How are you?'. He could have gone into the cubicle with a harsher tone, maybe even accusatory. But Luke, a decent man, appeared to retreat and become closed off if someone directly confronted him like that from the beginning. Going too far in the other direction would probably have been just as bad, maybe even worse. Asking about work is right out, that would only mentally link the issue at hand to his performance and cause an even bigger issue down the line. In the end, 'How are you?' won out, the simplicity and non confrontational approach would work with Luke's personality.

It actually seemed to work. A little of Luke's color seemed to come back, and a confused look crept into his eyes.

"I… I'mmm. I'm fine sir."

"Have you tried that lunch truck everyone has been talking about recently?"

Luke's face calms down into a small smile, "If you mean the one two blocks up, Bob got me a burrito from it yesterday. It's just as good as everyone has said."

"I need to get over there." Seth walks just inside the cubicle and squats down to be closer to Luke. " I saw that you came back late from lunch today."

Luke's voice betrays him, "… I… umm."

Seth calmly says, "Don't worry, it's okay to take your time with lunch every now and then."

"I know, I'm sorry sir."

"It's okay. Just try not to make it a habit, otherwise your fellow workers have to make up for your tardiness and that's not fair to them."

Luke thinks of Bill in the next cubicle over. Making him work harder just because of his selfishness isn't right. It just wasn't Christian.

"Listen, I'm not even going to make a note of this talk. You're a hard worker and I can see that you aren't doing this maliciously. As well, I haven't heard any complaints since the last time we talked and that goes a long way with me."

Some of Luke's co-workers had complained about him openly talking about religion. Some had seen it as evangelizing and had taken offense. Luke was shocked at the news when Seth told him about the issue. He never felt like he discussed religion with anyone that wasn't specifically okay with the discussion. That being so, he was careful to keep religion out of the workplace.

"Thanks. I appreciate the understanding. I won't let you down."

A smile spreads across Seth's face. While beginning to stand up, he talks just loud enough for some of those in the surrounding cubicles to hear him. "That settles it, I'm just gonna have to go on my lunch break tomorrow. That lunch truck sounds worth it."

It took Luke a second to understand. "Oh, yeah it really is. Their burrito was hands down the best I've ever had."

"Well, I should get back to work. I'll see you around," says Seth as he strolls around the corner of the cubicle and back to his office.

Luke is stunned... Everything's fine. Today is definitely the last time he's going to church on his lunch break; but other than that, he got off amazingly well. An ever so small smile creeps onto Luke's face.

"Man, it sounds like someone's about to get a promotion."

This knocked Luke out of his stupor. He looked over to the cubicle door and saw Bill in his rolling chair and a smile on his face. "Nahhh, I bet you he tries to do that with everyone from time to time."

"Hey, no complaints here. Just remember who your friends are when you're 'looking down from on high'. I always wanted to ride someone's coattails."

Jokingly, Luke sighs, " Oh, you'll always have a place getting me my morning coffee."

"Oh yeah, I know. Hot, black, and two spits." And with a little chuckle, Bill goes back around to his own cubicle.

Luke's smile fades a little. He decides he has been given an amazing chance to change. Squandering such a chance wouldn't only hurt personally, but may keep Seth from helping others in the same way. Luke rolls back to his computer and gets back to work.

WASTE

Chapter 3

Light shines through the buildings, beautiful refractions bounce off windows and smear in the chalky red of brick. Dull gray lines combine into fire escapes, scaling the sides of buildings as if they were in a century-long symbiotic relationship between two giants. Dotting along the way up the building are a technicolor series of windows; some are open with curtains flowing out over the windowsill waiting for the wind to blow. Others are in stasis, unmoving, locked behind glass. Still, there is one. A window dull and flat, covered by a patchwork of cardboard bottoms from Chinese takeout bags and duct tape.

Inside the apartment, only a slight haze of gray light shines through the duct tape. A round kitchen table covered in old magazines and pizza boxes. Half a pot of coffee has been sitting on the counter for the better part of two weeks. Crowding one corner in the kitchen are brown boxes from old deliveries with even more boxes stacked inside. Dust lightly covers a sink overflowing with pots from past meals.

Soft fluorescent glow illuminates the hallway in slowly changing bands of green and purple. The glow is coming from the rear bedroom. Past the bathroom with the toothpaste stained sink and a towel that's pulled double duty as both bath and hand towel for the past three weeks. In the room sits a man clacking away at a keyboard and mouse. Rapidly moving with shifting colors dancing on his face. The glow of the monitor works with his patchy beard that refuses to come in all at once, making his face look thinner. His eyes seem to have glazed over in the way where someone doesn't need to focus on one thing at a time, but instead can see the entire image in front of them. This is the intent stare developed from years of a prolonged love of games.

Wyatt would tell you he has lived in this apartment for a year and a half, the only problem with that being, that it's a lie. He has lived here for four years but doesn't realize so much time has passed. In the years of forgotten time after graduating from high school, he tried an online college. Some would have done this to better themselves; others might do it so they didn't need to grow up as fast. Wyatt chose college so that his parents would help him with the rent. He only lasted three months. During that time, he found he could make enough money to pay for food and a better computer if he worked while he did his classes.

A large red clock counts down on the second monitor showing that there are twenty-two more minutes left.

Because of being an 'online college', every student needed to have a working computer. They needed to keep students from using technical issues as an excuse for being late with assignments. So every student was required to sign up with an approved tech support company off of a list. When Wyatt signed up for one, he found out that they were looking for knowledgeable people to work as tech support in their off hours for extra cash. So instead of working on schoolwork, Wyatt helped people with their computer problems. It started out as thirty minutes to an hour a day for three days a week. After five weeks, he was working between five and eight hours a day, every day. By the time three months came around, Wyatt was working so much that he could afford to pay all of his bills and then some.

Red numbers display that sixteen minutes remain.

After dropping out of college, what little time Wyatt had

been putting into school work could now be spent on gaming. Wood elves and war zones took most of his time when he wasn't helping someone figure out why "My computer keeps saying that my printer can't be found," or "I don't remember the password, do I really need it?" Time in games made a sort of skinner box, where dealing with people caused a negative reaction and playing the games to get away from people caused joy. Wyatt was making the little interaction he had with people into an intensely negative one.

Twelve minutes.

After a while, he used the game as the proverbial carrot. As long as he worked for eight hours every weekday and four hours on Saturdays and Sundays, he would give himself free rein to play as much as he wanted. This caused an issue of sleep deprivation as Wyatt stayed up for almost twenty hours every day and then slept as little as four hours just so that he could continue playing as long as possible.

Six.

Keeping a schedule became less important as time went on. Innovative websites allowed for Wyatt to purchase anything he needed off the internet and have it delivered to his door any time he wanted. Allowing Wyatt to sleep, eat, and play games whenever he wanted for however long he decided was enough.

Red LEDs count down to five minutes and flash a bright white. Wyatt just barely glances over to his second monitor and begins to logout of his game. After the game window closes, he takes an empty soda can from the desk, shakes it to make sure it's actually empty, and then tosses it into the open trash can in the room's corner. Aluminum cans clatter together as the new can meet with his brothers in the half full trash can as Wyatt delaminates himself from his chair to stand up. Popping and cracks reverberate through his body as he reaches for the mini fridge door to get another cold soda and a bag of almonds, then puts them down at the computer.

As time went on, Wyatt had to make a choice about how long and when he played his games versus worked. He could work as many hours that he wanted to, but only during the hours the hotline was open and for only a set hourly wage. So, eventually Wyatt opened up his own business. He now has two phone lines, one that all of his calls for the company he works for come in on and a second one that he purchased himself. Now he can charge a higher amount than he would receive on an hourly basis. Wyatt even had some customers that would call during emergency hours, paying double the normal rate just to get the problem fixed right away.

Wyatt goes down the hall to the bathroom to relieve himself. After a short time and a flush of the toilet, he comes back to his seat. Lowering himself gently down into the chair until he gets about fourteen inches from the cushion and then gravity takes over. Landing on the chair causes it to tilt back until it reaches its prime; unable to arch any further, a single wheel of the chair raises less than an eighth of an inch off the ground.

Forty-nine seconds.

He checks his email account for any new messages while putting his headset on. The two new messages he received were both spam.

The alarm goes off.

Wyatt closes out of his email and mouses over to an icon with the title of "Work Time". After clicking the icon, the screen goes black for a few seconds. White text appears over a black background, lines of code write themself into existence. The screen is now tiled into segments. The left half of the screen is a list of actions such as new call, hold, and time sheet. Each of the items in the interface has a picture associated with them. On the top right of the screen is a search bar to comb the internet for any information on an unknown issue. Under the search window are two clocks: a red clock that's already been counting down from four hours and a green clock that is frozen at zero. Wyatt made this interface to make his job easier; the left-hand side is the standard window his company makes all of their employees use. It allows the user to do anything they need to help the client, including step-by-step instructions for how to solve any issue the customer might have. Only problem with the step-by-step guides is that it usually takes forever and doesn't account for a realistic understanding of problems.

The mouse scrolls over to the "new call" button and clicks. Moments later a click from the headset and Wyatt goes into customer service mode.

"Hello and thank you for using 'Electric Bug-aloo'. What seems to be the problem with your computer today?"

"Oh, yes... My niece came over to my house today to print out a report for her English class. When she got out here it didn't want to print."

"Is this a desktop or a laptop?"

"Oh, she has this beautiful new laptop that her father got her for graduating from high school. She wanted a Dell, but her Dad found a deal on some other brand that starts with an 'A' but for the life of me I can never say the name of it correctly."

"That's fine, let's start by..."

For the next few hours, Wyatt helped thirty-two different callers with a wide variety of issues. Seventeen calls in, Wyatt was beginning to feel depressed. Each caller seemed to have something to care about, something that would make them worse off if it was gone the next day. Parents that worry about the photos of their children they never backed up, children that lose their music, or grandparents who can't video chat with relatives.

After caller number twenty-three, the same depression that was just hovering a few minutes before had landed like a solid rock of emotional turmoil. Caller after caller just seemed to intensify the self hatred Wyatt was feeling. Self reflection became constant and cruel as each of the people calling always seemed happier than he had ever been. Even when the caller was irate or even purposely being hurtful, they seemed to have a level of feelings that he never seemed to possess. Wyatt felt as if he had actually failed at feeling miserable.

By the last caller, Wyatt's clock had counted down to almost three minutes. Every second with this woman felt like she was laughing at him, telling him that his life was a joke and that she would have killed herself if she ever ended up like him. The way she talked about the photos she lost and how they were very important vacation photos that they got on a very expensive trip to Italy. But she believed it would be okay if they weren't found because it would give them an excuse to go to Italy again. This sunk Wyatt even further. Wyatt didn't have the money to go to Italy, nor the friends that would go with him, and definitely not the money to throw away on a second trip just to get some photos.

A part of Wyatt knew that this was completely uncalled for. Hours from now, he would tell himself that he was just stressed and overworked, that the people and situations he was being so unnecessarily hostile about were just harmless small talk and they didn't mean to be condescending.

"Hello?"

"Hmm… Oh, sorry about that. I seemed to have zoned out there for just a little bit."

Wyatt darted his eyes to his notes section and made sure that they had finished the repair.

"Is there anything else I could help you with?"

"Oh that's okay, I do that at the supermarket all that time. Why, one time, my husband Frank, he said that I looked at some cans of soup for almost five minutes."

She gave a small chuckle. Wyatt had learned that it was easier if he just went along with any laughter, so he laughed a little as well.

"Thank you, ma'am is there anything else I can help you with?

"Oh, no dear. I think we solved the problem."

"Okay then, I hope you have a nice rest of your day and thanks again for calling 'Electric Bug-aloo', please don't hesitate to call again."

A soft click and then silence with the hum from a running computer in the background let him know that the connection was severed. Glancing to the right showed a red clock that had reached zero, with a new button flashing over the red clock. Pressing the new button logged him out of the work client. Mousing over to the game icon seems to take all of his effort, but he opens the game, resets his clock and logs in from muscle memory. Bright colors of the game world fill the screen. A man in armor stands at attention, and other characters are moving around the lone man standing still.

Wyatt moves his hands off of the mouse and keyboard.

Hordes of characters move around the still unmoving man in the middle of the crowd. Red numbers count down and tick away.

Alone. In the game, no one cares. In life, no one sees.

And still, time is counting down.

HABIT

Chapter 4

Coffee was always an important escape for Henry. Each cup seemed to calm him down and allow his thoughts and feelings to come more easily. A cup could mean the start of a great day, as long as the brew was made well. If a cup 'was' made well, the tension from the day before just seemed to fall off his bones; while a bad cup could cement them in place to send the day into a dark spiral.

Henry is sitting in a large backed chair, sipping on a mug of freshly brewed coffee, one cream two sugars, and listening to all the conversations flowing around him. It makes for a great day. Henry first discovered this shop when he was sent to install cable in the back office. Some customers will offer water or juice if they're nice, instead, this owner made probably the most delicious cup of coffee he had ever had. She sat there talking with him about how she special orders all of their beans and how they keep the machines in top shape. After that, Henry was hooked. Anytime he was in the area and had some time to spare, he knew he could sit back in one of these chairs, pull up a mug, and improve his day.

"Oh, guess I need a fresh cup," says Henry as he stands up from his chair.

Walking to get in line, he sees the day's paper sitting on a table with no one around. He grabs the paper as he walks by to read it once he sits back down. Henry gets in line behind two people, one of which seems to have trouble ordering a simple coffee.

"Come on lady, it's not rocket science," he mutters under his breath.

Eventually, after what seemed like ten minutes of indecision, the line moved and Henry was next in line. Thankfully, she already knew what he wanted to order.

"Hey Henry, ready for your second cup?"

"Yeah I think my next appointment can wait a few minutes while I get to drink the best coffee in the city."

"Ohhh, I bet you tell all the baristas that," she says with a small chuckle and a flip of the hand.

They both chuckle a bit as she passes Henry a new cup with milk and sugar already added. "Thanks, Jane."

Henry goes to sit back down with his newspaper under his arm. The soft cushion gives way to his slightly bony frame. Rocking back, being enveloped into the cushion, letting the large chair take the weight of his body. Relaxation takes him into his own world, the warmth of the cushions from before he last got up spreading warmth back into him. Flexing his back, tensing his muscles, and closing his eyes to the warm embrace of the chair. Sipping the fresh mug of coffee adds a delicious taste into the mix that allows Henry to slip away from the city while he sits right in the middle of it.

Henry puts his coffee cup down so he can open up the paper. Searching for an article to read, he turns page after page. One article about tornadoes almost piqued his interest until he realized it was about how "Climate Change" was going to alter this thing or that. Not that he could get away with telling anyone what he really thought about climate change. He once told a client about how he didn't think it was real, and she insulted him for the next 20 minutes. After that, Henry kept his political views to himself and God.

Finding nothing else in the paper, he went back and read the story about tornadoes. As the article droned on about pressure systems, Henry's eyes hazed. The warmth of the chair adding itself to the sleeping spell. The quiet conversations seem to give the hum of white noise.

Bzzzzz... Goes Henry's phone, waking him from slumber. It seemed to happen more and more recently that he would doze off in one of these chairs. That's why he started setting alarms that went off every fifteen minutes for his break. He checked the clock to ensure he hadn't slept through any alarms, realizing he only had fourteen minutes left of his break.

Flexing his shoulders, Henry pops a stiff joint and feels the rush of relaxation that floods into the joint. Rotating the neck in an almost serpentine movement doesn't pop anything, but it loosens up the neck a bit. Fully awakened again, Henry picks up the mug of coffee that still radiates with the warmth of a fresh pour. Sipping the coffee lets a stream of warm heat wash throughout his neck and chest. The heat radiates pleasure as it spreads through the body, flowing down with the current of the liquid.

Sitting there in the coffee shop Henry loves to frequent. Henry's mind is making connections in his subconscious between the warmth flooding his body and the overall pleasure of the moment. With all of these factors, Henry can feel himself get hard.

Pants feeling tight cause Henry to shift a little in his chair. Thankfully, the large chair makes it difficult for anyone to notice, but just in case, he folds the newspaper up and puts it in his lap. More relaxed about the situation, Henry thinks about how he has been a lot hornier recently. Jessica has been asking for him to swing by her apartment a lot more in the past few weeks.

Such a young girlfriend has made him seem to come alive again. They've had sex sixteen times in the last ten days, and that would have been unthinkable even a few months ago. Would he have enough time to swing by now? She would be up for it. As soon as he was through the door, she would try to take his pants off. Hell, if he called her up on the way to her apartment, she would probably wait on the bed spread eagle and get herself started.

Thinking of the tight, youthful body on the bed with her hand sopping wet from her juices made Henry even harder. A shiver goes down his spine as he thinks about her silky smooth voice pouting that he made her wait so long for his rock hard cock. Asking for him to get on top of her, begging for him to fill her up.

Bzzzzz.

"...Aaaaa," exhaling Henry realizes he needs to get back to work. Even though it would be soooo sweet to take off now, he can't leave on company time. "You have to respect the work," he silently says to himself.

He double checks that his now half hard member won't show before he stands up. On the way to the door, he puts the newspaper on a counter for someone else to read. Maybe they will actually want to read some of that dribble those so-called "journalists" have been writing.

Opening the door to the coffee shop seems to add a modicum of noise as the hustle and bustle of the street adds itself to the clinking and chatting of the shop. But as the door closes on the shop, no noise seems to be lost.

On the way back to the van, he gets a call from the office.

Answering, he asks, "Henry here, how can I help?"

"Hi Henry, it's Seth from the office. Are you busy right now?"

Seth... Wasn't that the new manager that took over the branch? "No sir, I just got off of a break and was heading back to the van now."

"Excellent, can you come see me whenever you get back to

the office. I wanted to speak with you in person."

"Sure thing, when my shift ends I'll head that way."

"Okay, I'll see you when you get here. Goodbye."

He had hung up so abruptly that it took Henry a moment to realize that the line was already dead. "Oh... Okay."

Before he could put his phone away, Henry realized he was probably going to be late getting back today because of his talk with Seth. So he sent a text to Jessica.

Henry: I'm not going to be able to swing by today, but i'll make it up to you later this week

She texts back fairly fast

Jessica: awww □ what am i going to do without you

Jessica: i guess the new toy that came in the mail yesterday will have to do □ ♥

Jessica: i was hoping you could use it on me today □ maybe tomorrow □

Henry: Oh? Now I'll have even more of a reason to come over.

Jessica: oh yes □ but where are YOU going to cum?

Henry chuckled a bit to himself. Jessica knew exactly how to push his buttons. Well... the only button she ever seemed to press, or want to press, was the one for a rock hard cock. But that only meant she seemed to know that button by heart at this point.

Getting back in the van, Henry realized he needed to send one more text.

Henry: Hun I'm going to be a little late today. The boss wants to see me in his office after work and I don't know how long it will take.

The reply came almost as fast as the others.

Kim: Sure thing, I'll push on starting dinner a little. That way, it will be ready when you get home.

Kim: He's probably going to thank you for working late so many times these past few weeks. I love you.

Henry: love you too

That last text made Henry stop. He did love her. Then why was he so enthralled with Jessica? Did a twenty-three-year-old really make him happier than the wife he's had for twenty-four years? It's not like he didn't love his wife. Hell, if you were to ask, Henry would tell you that his wife was definitely more beautiful in her youth than Jessica ever was. And that's not to say that she wasn't beautiful now either. Kim liked to take care of herself, going to the gym four times a week and watching what she ate kept her fitter than all but the most active for their age range.

But beauty doesn't stop a relationship from going stale. Good looks don't keep a person happy if they feel the other person is drifting further away.

"Why does it have to be this complicated?"

The love of his life is waiting for him at their house, ready to cook him a meal for his tired body. Why is it her fault for not being able to be young and different? Why should he be chasing the youth that he'll never get back? Maybe it was because he wasn't in love with his wife any longer... These questions and more swam through Henry's mind as fast as the answer left his lips.

"No."

He still loved her, he loved the way she looked at him on Sunday mornings when he surprised her with coffee in bed. He adored the way she drew little circles in the corners of any paper she was writing on while trying to think. She did so much for him; she seemed to live every day to make sure that he had what he needed in life.

Then why was he unable to stay faithful? He had never

cheated on his wife before Jessica; but even in the height of the physical pleasure Jessica could give to Henry, he had never wanted to break things off with Kim.

"Choosing one is the issue… Oh well, I don't have to choose now."

Pulling out his phone, Henry calls up dispatch for his next appointment.

HARSH SINCERITY

Chapter 5

Clicking of keys on a keyboard makes a melodious white noise in Seth's office. The report he was working on, for the higher-ups that sent him to this branch, was taking form in front of him. Such long reports were useless in his mind, but explaining as many things in as much detail as possible seemed to cut down on the misunderstandings that were bound to pop up. One time, he sent a one paragraph report on the fact that everything was progressing without a hitch. He would never repeat that mistake again. During the next three days, numerous higher-ups repeatedly called, requesting information on various topics already thoroughly discussed and resolved. To prevent this from happening again, Seth acted as if he had never given a single report since starting at a new location. There was some cutting of information that was required just so that the email wasn't twenty pages long, but trimming down was always much easier than bulking up.

In the middle of a sentence about a manager he fired two weeks ago, the computer froze. Lines of pixelated lightning seemed to be frozen across the monitor. A sigh escaped Seth's mouth as he rolled his eyes in frustration.

Thump. Thump.

After smacking the monitor a little out of frustration, Seth takes his other hand off the keyboard and puts both hands through his hair.

"I can't believe this is happening again," he said, while leaning back in his chair to look at the ceiling.

The computer had been getting worse over the past few hours. It seemed like the pauses kept getting longer, as well as more frequent. Even the IT guy that was sent over didn't know what to do, he never saw the issue first hand, thought the issue was a loose cable, searched for forty-five minutes and then left before it started having issues again.

Glancing down at the screen again showed a blinking line on the word document where the next words should be typed. Giving a silent thanks to whoever helped this time, Seth moved his hand to the mouse and saved the report before the computer crashed in a glitchy mess again. Seth was never that good with electronics. He knew enough about office programs for work, but never enough to have considered himself fluent. He mainly knew how to type, search for things online, and to smack a device when it decided not to work.

"Now if only I could get my phone to start behaving."

After the computer finished saving, he went to type. But before he could begin, a knocking at the door diverted his attention.

"Come in."

The door opens to reveal Henry.

"Oh, Henry. Can you shut the door on your way in? There were a few things I wanted to talk about," as Seth gestures to a seat on the other side of his desk.

"Sure thing, what did you want to talk about?"

Knowing that the only thing he knows about Henry outside of work is that he's married, Seth asks, "Not too much... How's the wife?"

"She's just fine, thanks for asking."

Smiling, Seth says, "I know about the coffee shop you stop at while you're still on the clock."

Henry's expression doesn't change. He doesn't move or show any sign that what Seth just said had any effect. Seth made a mental note **not** to play poker against Henry.

"Do you have anything to say in your defense?"

"Not really. I've never made it a secret that I take breaks. The large majority of my pay comes from on-site sales of equipment and then installing that equipment in a timely manner. The more I can sell and set up in a shorter amount of time means the more I make. The small amount of hourly pay I do receive is, in essence, is there to make sure that I'm covered by minimum wage laws."

"While that is true to a certain extent, you seem to be taking advantage of the situation. There are days that you have spent three hours at the coffee shop. That is beyond a simple break. It shows a lack of respect for the job, and for the company paying you to sit and drink coffee."

Henry's face relaxes and falls a bit. After a long but soft sigh he says, "You're right, I guess I had been so caught up with the fact that you guys let me make my own hours so much, that I thought it would be alright."

Seth gives a mental sigh or relief, this had the chance of being a huge backfire. If Henry had made no concessions to the fact that he had essentially defrauded the company of money, things would have had to go down a much different road. Starting with the immediate termination of Henry and all the fallout that would entail. Henry is by far the best worker in his department, and could do the work of three new installers. Losing him would have meant pushing his plans for the division back by at least three months.

"What can I do?", asked Henry.

"**We** can do a lot for each other. Since you acknowledged the issue and seem to be up to change, **we** can help each other out."

A puzzled look comes over Henry's face.

"It's not that confusing.", says Seth, a little heated, "You don't even have to change what you're doing that much. Just call in your breaks to dispatch so that they know to mark it on your timesheet. Hell, if you make sure to do it right away, I'll even pay you 50% of your standard pay for the time you take off."

The confusion on Henry's face had changed to shock.

Seeing the shock, Seth continued, "You shouldn't be **that** surprised. You weren't that far off about the normal pay being low. It's also the least we could do for our number one installer."

"Thanks, I appreciate you letting me continue my routine."

"As long as you don't take advantage of the offer and keep your installs up, then I don't mind you taking your time. We are here to make money after all."

"I will sir. Is there anything else you need from me?"

Thinking about it for a second, Seth responds, "No, we covered all of the issues I was going to bring up."

Henry stands to leave. Walking to the door, he hears Seth say, "Damn it, not again." Along with a thumping sound from an open hand hitting a monitor.

"Is something wrong with your computer?"

"Yeah, it keeps freezing and wont do anything for a long time. Then it will suddenly either crash entirely or start working like nothing happened."

"Have you called..."

"The IT department, a few times to no avail. It takes them forever just to show up and the problem just keeps getting worse and worse."

Henry thinks for a second and then hesitantly says, "I know of a phone service that you could try. It can be a bit expensive for really long solutions because they charge by the minute. But, they only charge you if the issue gets fixed."

Henry hands Seth a business card

"Do they take long to show up?"

"Oh, no. They do remote login and over the phone repairs only. They do get busy sometimes, so you might have to wait in the phone queue."

"Thanks, I'll give them a try."

Henry leaves the office and breathes out an enormous sigh. Meanwhile, Seth continues to inspect the business card and places it on the desk for later.

"Aww shit..."

The computer had completely crashed this time.

"At least I saved my progress."

SEARCH FOR WISDOM

Chapter 6

Seth is leaning back in his chair as he looks out the window at the city's skyline. The tall vertical lines that rise from the ground and grasp for the open sky above always puts Seth at ease.

Most of the other office workers have left already. Those that remain are usually one of two types of people: bootlickers that want Seth to notice that they were still here after he had already left; or someone that honestly wanted to put in a good day's work and doesn't feel that they finished their goal. Thankfully, in the era of computers, figuring out which category someone falls into is as simple as checking a spreadsheet. Now, the spreadsheet doesn't tell you everything, like who's gaming the system by falsifying their entry and exits. It also helps that a good deal of people aren't willing to stay the extra two hours past normal clocking out time to try to outlast Seth. He learned a long time ago that if you come in thirty minutes early and stay at least one hour extra, you will eventually see almost everybody's comings and goings. And when the higher-ups call someone like him to clean up a division, it signals that there are significant areas for improvement.

Seth turns his chair halfway around so he can pick up his cellphones bluetooth headset and the card that Henry had given to him earlier. Dialing the number on the card, Seth leans back in his chair to wait for an automated message.

"Thank you for calling 'Wyatt's Junction Box', do you have a previous account with us already?"

"Oh, I wasn't expecting someone to be available right away... No, I haven't used this service before."

"I'm glad to hear that you weren't waiting long, sir. If you don't mind, we'll be taking a minute to get your account set up.."

After a few basic questions to set up the account and explain the issues Seth had been having, Wyatt gets permission to take control of the computer so that he could try to solve the problem.

"So this is a work computer?" Wyatt asked, while simultaneously typing up notes.

"Yeah, but it's been like this since I got transferred over to this office."

"Oh yeah? Did anyone tell you how long it's been like this?"

"Oh, no. The guy that used the office before me was transferred to another division before I showed up."

As they talk, Seth is watching the mouse scroll back and forth across the screen to open windows that Seth never knew existed. But here is someone that knows these windows like the back of his hand to where the mouse is almost never paused for more than a few seconds.

"I can't believe how good you are at this," said Seth, amazed.

"Yeah, I always loved computers and figuring out how they worked. So this kind of job just seemed to make sense at the end of the day."

Even while talking, the mouse movements never seemed to slow down or stop for very long. There were even times that the speed seemed to increase for a bit.

Wyatt asks, "What kind of work do you do?"

"Oh, I like to think of myself as a corporate fixer. I'm usually called into a division when something has gone terribly wrong and needs a new set of eyes to trim the fat and get the rest of the people back to work."

"Sounds exhausting."

"You're not wrong, and I'm the youngest person this high up in the company's history. But... I mean, the pay is great. The benefits are worth it, and I get to see new cities on a fairly regular basis. But, in the end, this job is just a means to an end."

"How so?"

"Well. I like what I do, and I like being able to help the outstanding employees thrive. But, I've never found anything at work that would make me want to stay in any one place. Hell. Most of the time I go out and party just to be able to have any sort of fun."

The mouse stutters to a stop for a second and then Wyatt asks, "Wait... Party?", as the mouse on the screen moves again.

"Oh yeah. Nothing too crazy, but I love the nightlife in a big city. The clubs being packed together and the thumping of the music always make me feel alive. Half the reason I was willing to get so high in the company was so that I would have the freedom to live however I wanted. A nice house and a nice car are good to own, but I could have stayed much lower in the organization if all I wanted was a decent place to live and a good car. I wanted the ability to do whatever I wanted, whenever I wanted. And it just so happened that I was amazing at clearing out the useless people in a company and getting the rest back up to speed."

Wyatt stopped. He knew he shouldn't ask the question. It wasn't professional. He didn't want to alienate a client... but he had to know.

"Does going out... I mean. Does having that freedom keep you from feeling alone?"

They were both silent. The only thing either of them could hear was the humming of their computer fans. Then the mouse on Seth's screen started moving again.

"I'm sorry, I don't know why I asked that. It was inappropriate."

"No no no,it's... it's okay. It just caught me off guard. I... I don't know if I've ever really felt alone. I'm usually working or partying so much that other relationships never seemed to matter."

A few moments go by, and Wyatt comes back and says, "Well, it looks like I'm done here. You had some bad malware hiding in a connection to your printer, but I was able to get it cleared out and solved for you easy enough. Was there anything else I can help you with?"

Coming back to his senses, Seth says, "No, this was great... thanks for the turnaround."

"Not a problem sir. If you keep having the same issue, make sure to give us a call. Thank you for calling Wyatts Junction Box, have a nice day."

"Thanks, I'll do just that," said Seth, before hanging up.

Seth leans back in his chair, still thinking of what the man on the phone had said. About how his life had been up till now. After college, he immediately started working, and a high-level executive quickly took him on as a protégé. Once he finished a few years of grueling nonstop work, his mentor sent him to a distant branch that had been a major problem for some time. Months of work, firing dozens of people, and conducting thousands of one-on-one meetings with valuable employees, Seth had saved the branch from closure. Seth's mentor let it slip later on that all the company's top brass expected him to fail and learn that sometimes there is nothing you can do. After that, they sent Seth from failing branch to failing branch. Never once staying long enough to really make any lasting friends outside of work, and part of that was Seth knowing that he would be at a new branch before long. It's been fun, moving from place to place. Exploring the nightlife and clubs of different cities all across the nation. Each city was different, and the freedom to explore was exhilarating enough to make Seth never want it to end. But it would have to end sometime... right?

Wyatt was also leaning back in his chair. Comparing his meager life to Seths. They both seemed to do exactly what they had wanted to do with their lives, but even then, Wyatt knew that both of their happiness seemed to be skin deep. He knew that nothing that he did would matter. No one would care about him if he left this apartment today and never returned. Even his family felt distant and cold. He knew his parents loved him and wanted what was good for him, but they never seemed to understand what he wanted or talked about. So, slowly over time, they stopped talking. They would email or text now and then, but even then, they just never seemed to understand his point of view. He felt so alone in the world.

A blinking red light.

Wyatt sniffs away the sadness that was creeping itself in. Instead, he prepares for another caller.

"Thank you for calling 'Wyatt's Junction Box', do you have a previous account with us already?"

WITHERED LAMENT

Chapter 7

Luke sits in his pew. He hurried here after work and proceeded to get lost in reading passages of the bible. As time goes on, Luke's mind wanders. He thinks about the church and why he feels the need to come to this place so much. Why does he seem to be bound to come to this building day after day after day? Why does the church call to him as it does?

Such thoughts, and the silence that comes with them, are broken by the creaking of the church's front door. Luke shakes the arrant thoughts out of his head and the fog of negativity vanishes once again. Luke sees someone new walk through the doors, letting in the noise of the street.

Wyatt is nervous. He's known the location of this church for years and even walked past it a few times during holiday service. But he doesn't know why, today of all days, he walked inside. Wyatt looks around the church, hoping to find someone that could help him, but he can feel his face lose blood as he realizes that there seems to only be one person in the church and that they are looking his way. Is he doing something wrong? Are you not supposed to stand here?

"I knew this was a mistake, I can't do anything right," Wyatt says under his breath.

Luke sees an obviously lost man that seems a bit scared and

flustered. He wants to see if he can help. Luke slowly gets out of his pew and gently walks over to the man.

Oh, no. Why is that man coming over to me? I knew I did something wrong. Maybe the church is only for their congregation. Do they expect me to pay for a membership?

"Hello. I haven't seen you at service. Are you new to the area and looking for a church?"

"Oh... Uhhhmmm. Nno. I live around the corner. Um that way and. And I knew about the church. It's such a beautiful church, but I never thought... Well that is... I've never been in a church before..."

"Oh, well we're always open to anyone that wishes to join the flock, or if you just want to pray a bit, even if you're just trying to learn, or... if you just need to talk?"

His lack of awareness of how obvious he was being embarrassed Wyatt, and he said, "Oh, that's good to know. Well, I guess I'll get going now."

"No, please. Stay a bit. It seems like you're having a hard time with something, and I know that it can be hard to talk with those we love about our problems. So why not talk with me? I might not be a priest, but I'll promise not to talk about whatever you say."

Wyatt stops for a bit and then agrees. Luke leads Wyatt over to a pew for them to sit down.

"So, what made you think of coming to church?"

"I... I'm not really sure. I've been feeling like my life hasn't meant anything. That I seem to wake up every day with no other reason than to work. Even the things that I used to do for fun have turned into a sort of job that I barely enjoy anymore."

"Do you think that the church will give you meaning?"

Wyatt is stunned and, after a few seconds, says, "No, I guess not. I just remember stories that I've heard of people finding God later in life and that their entire outlook on life was changed for the better."

"Well, we can help. But, you need to be the one to do the hard work in making your life better. What we excel in is providing love and guidance for those that need it."

"But… I just want to find a place that I'll belong. I wake up in a dirty apartment because I barely have the time to clean. I eat junk food because I don't know how to cook for myself. Hell, the last time I asked a girl out was years ago because when I did, she openly made fun of me until I wanted to go home and die. I never felt like my life was important. The only people that showed me any sort of unconditional love was my parents, and even then, it was mainly my mom. That's not to say that my dad doesn't love me, but he's been so distant that I'm sure he sees me as a disappointment and a giant waste of space."

"I'm sure he loves you," Luke interjects.

"Does he? I haven't seen him smile in front of me in the past 5 years. He's always busy with work or a friend. He's never made time for me. I remember him giving me a computer for my birthday when I was young, and saying that it should keep me out of his hair. All I wanted was to make him proud. So I learned to use the computer.I learned everything that I could so that I could make him proud and make sure not to bother him. Then one day, he told me that I spent too much time on the computer and to go outside and get a life. I got bullied outside, I was ridiculed outside, why would I ever want to go there? And now I stay in my apartment for days at a time. I rarely need to go out for anything. But recently, the apartment seems so small and stale. I seem to be on the knife's edge, waiting for something to happen and push me over. My life seems worthless and dull, and I almost want it to end."

Luke sees the glinting of water around the edges of Wyatt's eyes, "I'm sorry to hear that. And I wish that there was something that I could say that I could guarantee would solve your issues. But I'm not doing so well myself."

"What do you mean?"

Luke exhales and then continues, "I've been coming here more and more recently. I seem to be here more than I'm at home nowadays. I used to get so much out of going to church, the love and affection, the sense of community that made getting through the week bearable. Now... Now I still feel those things from the congregation, but they don't fill me up like they used to."

"Then why do you still come back? Isn't it all useless?"

"No. The love is still there. The community is still here. I just feel like this is a test. This empty feeling that keeps me from God's love and joy like I used... it'll go away."

"How do you know?", questions Wyatt.

"I have faith."

They both sit there in the silence. Thinking over their conversation. But Luke remembers the time and looks to his watch for confirmation. "Oh, wow. Look at the time. I have to get going if I'm going to get dinner made by a reasonable time," Luke says as he rises and starts to walk away. About halfway out of the pew, he turns back to Wyatt and asks, "Do you need me to stay for a bit. Food can always wait."

"No. I'm fine. Thanks for the talk, it really means a lot. I might try to pray for a bit."

Luke smiles and nods before turning around to leave. As the door closes, bringing the church back to a place of silence, Wyatt puts his head down in a prayer. After a minute, Wyatt opens his eyes and feels embarrassed and self-conscious. He looks around to see if anyone has arrived to see him.

"What am I doing...?" he says under his breath. "I can't believe that I thought this would help."

But, even though he doesn't realize it, some of Wyatt's stress has dissipated. Wyatt stands straighter. And, with a bit more confidence than when he came into the church, he steps outside.

~MONDAY NIGHT~

DARE TO WANDER

Chapter 8

Walking back to his apartment, the sky turned orange and red; by the time Wyatt was inside, there was no more blue on the horizon.

Wyatt's mind keeps replaying his call with Seth, but he can barely remember their conversation or the actions that stemmed from it. He mainly just remembers how the conversation made him feel. He also remembers the busy sidewalk that he usually never has to walk on. The density of walkers rushing home before the light of the sun is lost behind buildings.

Hunger pains come across Wyatt as he realizes how little he's eaten this afternoon. So, almost without thinking, he grabs the phone and orders his standard order from his usual pizza place down the block. Even while placing the order, he can't help but think about how the phone call makes him feel. After ending the call, he decides to browse the web until the pizza's delivered.

Sitting down in his chair, he loads up a few websites that he normally likes to check. Searching for interesting stories or funny articles to pass the time. A video of a cat trying to smack someone in the face but falling off the counter instead. Two different articles that seemed to be reworded explanations of a political issue that happened last Saturday. Link after link after link. None of the sites or articles could hold Wyatt's interest. As time ticked by, he started scrolling without even reading the titles. About fifteen empty minutes later, the phone rings.

The abrupt sound startles Wyatt. That ringtone is his company line.

"I would really rather not right now."

But as the ringing continues, Wyatt remembers that he's technically during off hours, which means he can bill double per minute.

"Gahhh... Okay, maybe it'll take my mind off of things." So Wyatt grabs his headset, clicks over to his tech support program and answers with, "Thank you for calling 'Wyatt's Junction Box', do you have a previous account with us already?"

Sounds of music and talking in the background are all that Wyatt can hear. No one seemed to talk to him or even seemed to hear him. Instead, he can hear the laughing and talking of someone that seems to be thrilled. Then the music increases in volume enough to drown out the talking. Wyatt leans back in his chair while listening to the sounds of thumping music in the background. He takes about a minute to realize he doesn't even know who called him. So he takes the number and looks it up in his system. It's Seth, the man from earlier. He must have pocket dialed Wyatt by accident. He must be out living his life like we talked about.

Wyatt closes his eyes and tries to picture what Seth must be doing now. He imagines a handsome man sitting at a table across from a beautiful woman. Each of them sips their drinks as they tell each other stories and laugh. All the while, a horde of people are dancing to the music that's playing all around them. Wyatt's eyes fly open to the sound of someone knocking on his door.

"Huh? Oh, the pizza."

Wyatt hangs up the phone call, takes off his headphones, and goes to the door to pay for the pizza. Placing the pizza on the counter, he realizes how small and dull his apartment is. He knows that the only warmth in these rooms is coming from the hot pizza before him, but that only makes him more sad.

Something in Wyatt breaks loose. In his mind, there is nothing left for him if he doesn't make a change right here and now. He walks down the hall and into his bedroom, finds a pair of clean slacks he hasn't worn in years, and puts them on. Thankfully, they fit, a bit tight, but otherwise in decent condition. Looking at his shirts, he picks one of his nicer button up shirts that his mother made him buy years ago. He checks himself in the bathroom mirror and combs his hair a little before walking to the front door.

Hand on the doorknob ready to go out, he's struck by fear. Fear of the unknown of interacting with the world outside of this apartment. Even going out to the church earlier wasn't as scary as what Wyatt was planning to do. Actually wanting to go out, intending to meet new people with the potential of making friends. Or enemies. Why would anyone want to be friends with him? Why wouldn't they laugh at him and kick him out? He was worthless to other people. Everyone could see that he was worthless and worthy of ridicule.

But a different train of thought sparked. What did he have to lose? He didn't have any real friends in the city. If he made a friend tonight, then he would be infinitely better than if he didn't go out. In fact, the only bad thing that could happen is if no one wants to interact with him and that would leave him exactly where he is right now. So, why not try? Why not try for the change in the world that he wants to see?

Wyatt opens his front door and walks downstairs to the street and into the chilly night air. And as he walks down the street, he doesn't realize that he's walking with a little more pep in his step. Night has descended upon the city, but the street is alive with the glow of shops and headlights. Brisk air cools him down as he walks with nowhere in mind. At each intersection, he takes the path of least resistance and follows the flow that most people are taking. As the blocks go by, he gets winded, so Wyatt slips over towards the next alley to rest for a minute.

Wyatt hasn't had to walk that long or far in years, and while it felt amazing, he now also feels the pain of not working out for all these years. Standing just inside an alley, slightly panting from overheating, Wyatt looks back at the throng of people constantly streaming by the alley. Each person has their own place to be and their own life that they're living. Each of them doesn't know the criticism or accolades that they all go through daily. And here he is. So close to all of them, but he can only see them from afar.

The sound of clicking and soft talking comes from behind Wyatt. Slowly, he turns around, keeping his eyes on the people walking on the sidewalk as long as he can. When he finally drags his eyes away, they snap over to three young girls that entered the alley on the other side. All three girls wore small, colorful dresses and heels, dressed for a night out clubbing. They stop walking in front of the only other person in the alley, a fairly tall, well-dressed man that looks bored out of his mind. After fifteen seconds of talking and then thirty seconds of getting out their IDs to show the man, he lets them through the door. After making sure the door is closed properly, the man scans the area and sees Wyatt.

He nods a little and then asks, "You want to get in? There's a $20 cover for guys."

It takes Wyatt a second to realize that he should answer, "Uuuhhh, sure." Wyatt walks over to the man in front of the door. "What... what's it like in there?"

Moving closer makes Wyatt realize just how tall the other man is. Now right next to the man, he must seem miniscule while trying to take out his wallet.

"Oh. You know, tons of beautiful ladies wanting to dance. Tons of men trying to take the ladies home. And more alcohol than either of those groups could drink in a month."

The bouncer barely looks at Wyatt's ID, and instead is fast to take the $20 before he turns the knob on the door to let him inside. Walking past the man, Wyatt finds himself in a short hallway that makes a right-hand turn after a few feet. Halfway to the turn, Wyatt hears a click behind him and turns around quickly to see the back of the door that's now closed. Now a bit scared of being alone in a strange place, he continues to the turn in the hallway and peers around the corner. An extremely bored woman stands behind a counter with a sign that says 'coat check'. It takes a few seconds, but he realizes he doesn't have a coat to check, and that he must seem like the stupid one in this situation. So he continues on past the woman as he hears soft music becoming noticeable. As he follows the next bend around a corner, the music grows louder, and he periodically feels a slight bass tremble through the floor. Finally, Wyatt stands before another door. A door that seems to be the only thing holding back the music from flooding into the world behind him. And then. He steps through into a world of dancing lights and sound.

Beams of moving light bounce across the dancefloor illuminating the nameless faces all moving together to the beat of the music. A hoard of people, all having more fun in their own little world than Wyatt has had in years. The oppressive thumping and blaring of the song makes it obvious that Wyatt is trespassing in this space. Everyone must know that he doesn't belong here. Surely they can already tell. He needs to leave, before they confront him. Before something worse can happen. That's it. He'll leave. And then...

The crescendo breaks for a second and silence rules. That one second of tranquility jogs Wyatt out of his thoughts. He sees the 'hoard' of people on the dance floor all having fun, but he sees how few people there actually are. Even the bar and surrounding tables aren't as full as he initially thought. And then the music comes back with all of those on the dance floor following along with the song. Wyatt realizes that no one even knows he's here. They're all just here to have fun and be around people that also want to have fun. So, he takes a deep breath and walks towards the bar to order a drink.

Although the club isn't overcrowded, Wyatt finds it difficult to walk through the crowd. He finds himself confused by needing to backtrack around different groups of dancers and people at tables, which have completely blocked off certain walking areas. But, eventually, he makes it to the safety of the bar and lets out a very large breath while putting both of his hands onto the wood bar top. Looking down the bar, he sees a bartender talking to some girls asking for shots.

Wait. Now that he's in front of the bar, what does he want to drink? He looks at the racks upon racks of alcohol on the wall. None of them look familiar, and he has no reference for any of their names. Is whisky a good drink? Probably not a good idea to find out. What about wine? They probably don't sell a lot of wine. He doesn't want to look out of place. Beer is always a straightforward choice. But what brand? He looks around for anything saying what beers are available. Wait. What was that thing people always said on TV? Oh no, the bartender is coming this way. What do I do?

"What can I get for you tonight?"

"Uhhhhh. Whatever beer you have on tap?"

"Sure thing."

Wyatt sighs out an excessive amount of stress as the bartender turns to pour his beer. Such a simple little exercise that most people wouldn't have worried about, but here he is almost having a panic attack over ordering a drink. Wait. I still need to pay. Wasn't there another thing people say?

"Here you go, that will be $6. Do you want to start a tab?"

That was it. Starting a tab. So Wyatt gets out a credit card and hands it over. "Yes please."

The bartender nods and then walks away.

Turning around with a drink in his hand, Wyatt realizes he doesn't know what he should do next. Everyone else seems to be having fun dancing or talking. Taking a sip of beer to quiet his nerves, he needs to decide if staying at the bar is the best choice or if he should dive headfirst into the deep end by dancing. Was there a middle ground? How about finding a table first; he could drink his beer and think from there.

Moving gradually over to some booths and tall tables around the edges of the room. Wyatt finds couples holding hands and kissing, groups of friends laughing and talking together, and one table with someone standing by herself. At first glance, she's indistinguishable from anyone else in the club, but upon closer inspection, she seems out of place. As out of place as Wyatt feels. Seeing her like this, sipping her drink, he feels drawn to her.

Walking past a few tables, he makes his way to her and asks, "Hi, do you mind if I drink with you?"

She lights up upon seeing his face. Wyatt would have sworn that she seemed to recognize a bit of herself in him. The same thing that he felt from across the room.

"Sure, we should probably talk a bit as well. Otherwise it might get a bit awkward."

As he slides into one of the tall chairs, he says, "thanks, this my first time coming out like this and it's all a bit overwhelming."

Smiling at the innocent admission, she says, "anytime, I've come out a few times before, but it still feels a bit 'overwhelming'."

This is great, as the thoughts started swirling in his head. We can talk a bit and have some fun. Wait. Aren't I supposed to have done something else? What was it? Oh yeah. Putting his hand out to shake, he says, "My name's Wyatt."

She responds with, "Dawn, pleased to meet you, Wyatt."

Awkwardly, they shake hands as Wyatt replies, "And the same to you, Dawn."

They sip their drinks for a bit and then Dawn asks, "So you said this is your first time out. Why is that?"

"Oh. I was always a bit scared to come out. It always felt like I would step outside and then everyone would know that I wasn't meant to be there."

"But you're here now. So something must have happened that made you change things up."

"I... I got a call today. I did some tech support for a guy who talked about going out to clubs like this as if it was the only thing in the world that mattered to him. It made everything that I've done recently, or, well...the lack of things that I've done recently, put into perspective. I only ever left my apartment for trash or food. Even the time I spent doing things that I usually like has been boring lately."

"Sounds like you needed a change in your life. And you did it."

"Maybe, this could be the first step... Or the last." Wyatt looks down at the floor for a moment and then up again.

"Keep it up. It does get better."

"Oh yeah?" He could feel his heart begin to race.

Playfully she responds, "Yeah... I've been coming out at least once a month now since my therapist recommended it."

"That seems like an odd request from a therapist."

"A little. I have my own issues dealing with other people in situations that I couldn't control. So she recommended that I force myself into a place where I have less control over others trying to talk with me."

"Oh, really?" Wyatt was trying to dial in on just her words.

"Yep. And it's helped a lot. Some of the people that come up are creeps just trying to get into my pants, but oddly enough... Most of the people that want to talk to me are actually really nice.

They usually still want to get into my pants, but they're usually really nice about it. I did have to change my expectations, because the first few times a decent person tried to talk with me, I kept wondering when the other shoe would drop. But it never did."

"Sounds like you're doing a lot better now. Why are you still coming out?"

"My therapist wants me to work on going out on a more regular basis."

"Makes sense… I guess."

"You said that you did tech support. What's that like?

"Oh… It's probably as boring as most jobs. I have to help solve the same 20 problems all day. There are some times that I get a real problem, and then I can actually enjoy trying to solve it. But most of the time it comes down to turning the printer off and on. You would be amazed how many times I've had to explain that a computer needs to be plugged in to work." He chuckled a bit to himself and studied her face for a reaction.

"No way!" she says with a laugh, hand covering her mouth.

"Oh yeah. I thought it would be a one off the first time. But I've gotten that one more times than I care to count."

"Sounds like you've got a fine job. Definitely repetitive, but you seem to be good at it."

"Thanks." They both sip their drinks before Wyatt continues, "oh, what do you do?" He smiles, trying to cover some of the nervousness.

"I work at a coffee shop." He noticed just how warm her tone was when mentioning her work.

"Does that make you a barista?" A sly grin grew on his face.

"Actually! I was recently taught how to use the machine, I guess you can call me a barista."

As they smile, both seem to imagine that the room has become brighter. While the surrounding crowd gradually increases, and the music gets louder, they continue to talk as if no one else existed. Not expecting anything from each other, but the companionship that each of them has been longing for.

NOSTALGIA

Chapter 9

We find Nolan sitting in his living room armchair watching TV late into the night. A bright and clean room with more than a few decorative touches that make this a comfy home instead of a sterile house. The most cluttered spots being all the surfaces that seem filled to the edges with framed pictures of loved ones. Some snapshots of his children when they were younger, others of them as they grew up and into their adulthood, even more of the grandchildren at various ages. But, the most prominent are those of his wife. Nolan keeps them front and center to keep her face and memory alive in his mind. Nolan used to hate the clutter of photos, but since her passing, he's refused to alter anything that reminds him of her.

Nolan becomes bored with the show he's watching. They've been releasing subpar episodes since season three and have been limping along from momentum at this point. Glancing to the side, he sees a photo of his wife and smiles.

"I love you dear." With a sigh he continues, "I'm so glad that you passed first, I wouldn't want you to live through the pain of missing the person you love the most."

As he stares at the photo, his stomach growls.

"Welp, hunny. It looks like I need to get some food." He looks around the room feeling a bit stifled. "I should probably get some air, it'll do me good."

Nolan slowly gets out of his chair and gets ready for a quick shopping trip down the street. First, checking his shopping list to see what else he might want to pick up while he's out. Then he makes sure to bring his shopping bag. Lastly, he checks he has his phone, keys, and wallet. Nolan takes a moment to reminisce about how his wife would always ask whether he forgot them. It didn't matter that he hadn't forgotten to bring them for months or years. Invariably, the one time she didn't ask would be the time that he forgot his wallet. He used to cry a bit every time he thought about that after she passed, but it's now become a welcome memory that reminds Nolan of the type of person his wife was.

Slowly, he makes his way to street level; thankfully his hip isn't acting up. At each floor, he takes a few seconds to rest, not that he necessarily needs to, but just to make sure that he doesn't hurt himself accidentally. He'll always remember the time three years ago when he was sore for two weeks because he took the stairs too fast. Nolan has always prided himself on never having to learn the same lesson twice; his wife would tell you he frequently makes the same mistakes, just that he wouldn't ever admit to it.

Once on the street, he angles into the flow of people walking. It's late enough that the foot traffic can easily go around him if they want to go faster without potentially clipping him on the shoulder. Nolan actually prefers going out after rush hour, since he can usually move slower.

Moving along the sidewalk, he reminisces about the years it took for the building across the street to be renovated. The noise and delivery traffic of that renovation are all but a memory now. Nolan and his wife had long discussions about how the project would never end and that they would have to live next to constant construction for the rest of their lives. Now that building has the best apartments for four blocks, and the waiting list to get an apartment is a decade long. So much of the city has morphed slowly over the years.

"I can't wait to see what comes next," he whispers under his breath.

Nolan turns the corner and enters the bodega he likes to frequent. Walking up and down the aisles, he grabs a few items he knows he needs and a few that he doesn't. Going up to the front of the store to pay, Nolan realizes the clerk is someone he hasn't seen working here before. Too bad; Nolan always likes to talk with the night clerks for a bit. But hates to impose himself onto anyone that he hasn't already seen before, so now he'll need to wait until they see each other a few more times.

Back in the night air, Nolan stops for a bit and takes in a breath. The haze of light over the streets and the white noise of the city come together as a wave of peace washes over Nolan. He would never willingly choose to move away from the city. Not that those times that he went camping with the family or drove a few hours on a scenic route wasn't peaceful or worth the trouble. But after a few days, those types of trips always make Nolan jumpy and irritable. On the other hand, being in the concrete jungle of the city with all of its noises and crowds of people has always calmed Nolan down.

"That's enough daydreaming. Time to get back.", He says under his breath as Nolan walks back to his apartment.

On the walk back, he sees a woman that he recognizes from around the block. He calls for her to stop and says hello. Nolan was friends with her parents when she was growing up in the neighborhood and asks how she and the family are doing. She politely tells him about how the family is faring and that her parents would love to have him over for dinner some night. After a little more conversation, Nolan let her go on her way with the promise that he will call up her parents to set up a dinner.

As she walks away, he can't help but think of his children living their own lives. Both of them have children of their own and are too busy to visit with their old man. His eldest granddaughter recently graduated high school and enrolled in a college a few hours outside the city. Nolan knows that they have busy lives of their own and doesn't want to intrude or hassle them more than he already does. It used to be that they would welcome almost daily visits to help with chores and watching toddlers play. As the grandchildren grew up and started going to school, their parents didn't need as much help and it was more of an inconvenience for them. But now he gets little to no time with the children unless there's a holiday or birthday. As well, the time between visits seems longer and longer.

With a small shake of his head, Nolan reproaches himself. They have their own lives to live. What kind of father would I be if I blamed them for that?

He walks back to his apartment and stands at the bottom of the stairs leading up. As he reminds himself to take it slow going up the stairs, Nolan thinks of his wife and wishes that she was still around. He knows that she would have kept up with their children and grandchildren more than he has. She was amazing at that sort of thing. She would plan little outings or trips to malls that wouldn't take much time, but would also make it easy for everyone to catch up on daily life.

As Nolan makes it to his floor, he hears someone humming in the hallway. Looking around for the source of the noise leads him to seeing one of his neighbors standing in front of his door trying to unlock the deadbolt. But each time he's about to get the key in the lock, the man seems to fumble the keys a bit or drop them outright. Now only a few feet away and in front of his door, Nolan has to make a choice. He doesn't know the man that well. He's lived here for a while, but their paths have rarely crossed in that time. While he doesn't look like the type that is any real danger, Nolan realizes that such an issue wouldn't have mattered to his wife. She would've needed to make sure that he was okay before letting him go inside alone for the night.

With a bit of resignation in his voice, Nolan clears his throat and asks, "How you doin' neighbor?"

The obviously drunk man looks around a bit at the sudden intrusion. Noticing Nolan for the first time, he smiles and does a little wave that makes him look even more drunk. He rounds back uneasily towards the lock before responding, "Ooohhh. Hehe, I'm fine sir. Just trying to get inside."

"You can call me Nolan; I've seen you around but we've never been introduced. What's your name son?"

"My name's Wyatt. I would shake your hand, but I'm having enough trouble with my keys."

A WELCOME NEIGHBOR

Chapter 10

"You sure don't look like you're doing well. Just how many times have you dropped your keys?", asks Nolan.

"I'm… I'm fine, just had a bit too much to drink," Wyatt said with an obvious slur in his voice.

Wyatt turned to put his back against the wall. Once his weight rested against the wall, he let out an enormous sigh and his shoulders sank towards the floor as his entire body seemed to relax. He began to slide down the wall a bit before catching himself and stiffening up his legs to keep himself upright.

Nolan watches this entire tableau unfold and takes pity on the boy. "Okay. Here's the deal, **you** are going to come into my apartment, **I** am going to make us some coffee to sober you up, and we will get to know each other a bit better."

"Oh, no you don't need to do that. I'll just head off to bed."

"Son. I wasn't asking. You look like you need more help than you realize, and I would hate myself if something happened that I could prevent."

Wyatt wasn't expecting such an answer. The truth seemed

to whir around him like a confusing blur. He never expected anyone to care about him. At the beginning of the night, he didn't think anyone would care if he lived or died. But here he was just a few hours later and more people had acted like real friends to him than he has had in years. Wyatt stresses his muscles to get off of the wall and amble his way to the older man waiting by his now open door.

"Thank you," he said, just loud enough for Nolan to hear.

"Son, we all need help sometimes. If you want to thank me, then pay it forward when you can," he says, guiding Wyatt into the living room. "Now sit down on the couch while I brew up some coffee." Pointing to the couch, Nolan walks through the room and into the kitchen.

Looking around the room, Wyatt is taken aback by the impressive amount of framed photos that litter most of the flat surfaces in the living room. Making his way to the couch, he notices that a good portion of them are of children growing up through the years, as well as some newer photos of what look like grandchildren. Wyatt's mind buzzed with confusion, most of the photos showed the growth of children and grandchildren with no photos of Nolan unless he was in the background. But there were a sizable amount of photos with a woman that appears to be Nolan's wife, and unlike Nolan, many of those photos were of her exclusively. The fuzz in Wyatt's brain seemed to clear up for a second, as it all seemed to click into place. She was dead. And now the only way he can see her are these photos.

Nolan poked his head out from the kitchen and asked, "Do you take yours with cream and sugar?"

"Oh, yes please. Two sugars if you could."

"Sure thing."

Wyatt's mind races again as he looks over the photos. Each of them show the love of a family that Wyatt could only wish to experience. While he knew that his father 'loved' him, he couldn't tell you he ever really experienced his father showing his 'love' for Wyatt in any concrete way. In fact, he doubted his father even thought about him on any regular basis.

"I see you like my collection."

"Huh?" Wyatt says, as he does a startled little jump. "Oh… Yeah. I couldn't help but look."

"Yep, my kids are all grown up and even have kids of their own. My wife loved it every time she could add a new frame to the collection once they moved out on their own. It made her feel like a bit of them was still here with us."

Wyatt said nothing. He knew his drunken brain couldn't be trusted. Not unless he wanted to say something to ruin this peaceful moment.

"I miss her dearly. I just hope that I'll never forget her face."

"Is… is that why you added so many photos of her?"

"Mostly," Nolan gives Wyatt a mug of coffee as he continues. "I also think she would want to be remembered alongside her children and grandchildren."

"Has it been hard for you since she passed?"

"Ohhhh. It was harder at first. It's almost impossible to explain, but the common explanation of a hole in your heart that never seems to go away is close enough to the truth. I loved her with all of my heart, and I knew that she felt the same way about me. That being said, our hearts grew to love our children and then again for our grandchildren when they came along, that didn't lessen the love we had for each other, or cheapen the love we felt in general. But her passing made that love difficult to enjoy. The knowledge that the love I had for her would never be returned again, that she would never do any of those little things that made me happy, that I would do things that I only ever did to make her happy in vain because there would be no one to enjoy them like she did. All of that pain was there… and so much more. But over time, the pain gets blunted. Not because it lessens, not because it goes away. Instead, you just become used to it living within you. You find a way to go on, you find a way to survive the pain within your own heart." His eyes studied the ground for a time in contemplation.

"I'm sorry, I didn't mean to ask such a heavy question. You've been so nice." The words were still slightly slurred, but they felt sobering.

"Oh, that's not a problem at all. I've quelled the pain in my heart in my own way. But, I do believe in a bit of tit for tat. So how are your folks doing?"

"They're... They're both alive. We don't... talk all that much anymore."

"A busy life will do that. I do wish my kids would call or visit more than they do, but I also know that they have their own lives to live and that I can't always take up too much of their time."

"No... It's... It's a bit more than that. My father and I never really understood each other. I tried to stay out of his way more than anything else. I'm a disappointment to him." Wyatt could hear the sadness rising in his own voice.

"My granddaughter thought the same thing about my son in law. She always wondered why he was never satisfied with her grades or accomplishments. I mean she was never a rocket scientist, but she had a good head on her shoulders and never got in trouble."

"What happened?"

"Oh. One day I sat them both down. You see their family life had been bad for a while and everyone in the family knew it. But, no one was having them talk. They kept talking about each other instead of to each other. I was so frustrated with all of this back and forth that I sat them down for lunch together to get things out in the open."

"Wait seriously?"

"Oh yeah, I couldn't handle it anymore. They both cared for each other. They just didn't want to talk and 'make things worse'. So I told them how I saw things. How neither of them were to blame, but that neither of them were helping the situation either."

"Did it help?"

"Oh it took a while, and the staff probably wondered why we were there for so long, but it ended in them hugging it out. My son-in-law loves his children, but he has a hard time showing that love. And my granddaughter was always a strong-willed child that refused to change her mind. So when she convinced herself that he didn't love her, any small evidence to the contrary was pushed aside."

"So their relationship is better now?"

"A parent's relationship with their child will always be difficult to explain."

Wyatt tried to steady himself as he listed one way and then the other, but was still curious. "But they're at least talking now right?"

"Oh? Oh yeah. He still thinks that she could be getting better grades. But she got into a decent college and is going for a decent well-paying major, so he's been giving her some slack."

Laughing a bit, Wyatt shakes his head a little and then says, "I guess nothing's perfect."

In a fast and clipped voice, Nolan breathes, "nope."

Wyatt looks into the cup of coffee that he has been sipping on. He's almost done with the cup and knows that he should leave to not inconvenience Nolan anymore than he already has. But he also likes the old man and his outlook on life.

"Son. It looks like you might need some help."

Wyatt looks up into the eyes of Nolan. He knows that this

man is giving an olive branch, that all he wants to do is help.

But before Wyatt can get his thoughts straight, Nolan continues, "have you ever thought of taking the next step in your relationship with your father? Because you may not have realized if he thinks that he's already made the first step and is waiting for you to make the second."

This crashed into Wyatt, his mind spinning with emotions and thoughts that refused to straighten out. "But what if he doesn't care?"

With steel in his voice, Nolan replies, "then you know to cut ties. If your father doesn't truly love you, then it's better to excise the growth with him now before he can hurt you even more."

Wyatt's eyes widened at the underlying venom in Nolan's voice. He knew it wasn't aimed at him, but at those that have a child but mistreat them.

With a sigh; Nolan softly says, "Listen, we're all human in this world. And there are those that should never become parents. But you're not required to love someone that refuses to love you for who you are."

"Tha...Thank you sir. It means a lot." Whiffs of moisture began welling up in the corners of Wyatt's eyes.

"Not a problem, do you want any more coffee?"

A quick head turn was all he needed to wipe away the imperceptible tears and replies, "No... In fact, I should be getting back to my apartment."

"Well. If you would do one thing for me. Please get to bed; almost nothing good comes from being drunk and awake this late at night."

Laughing a bit, Wyatt agrees and heads towards the door. Before he leaves, Wyatt turns around and asks, "Sir... Would you like to have dinner later this week?"

Surprised by the offer, Nolan smiled as he agreed. "Sure. That sounds wonderful. I'm actually free Thursday."

Wyatt had to think about it for a second. Thursday was one of his guild's raid nights. A year ago, if given this choice between dinner with a neighbor and raiding, he would have immediately and **strongly** chosen raiding. But tonight showed Wyatt just how much of life he was missing. So with minimal delay, Wyatt agreed, and they set up a time to get together.

After leaving Nolan's apartment, Wyatt heads down the hall to his own front door. With a new and much more sober head on his shoulders, he's able to put the key into the lock on the first try and enter his apartment.

Nolan locks his front door and returns to the living room, where he collects the mugs. Taking them to the kitchen, he puts them in the sink gingerly so that he can wash them later. On the counter next to him, he finds the bags of groceries he had gone out to buy. It seemed like something that had happened so long ago. Nolan unpacks the bags and puts away the groceries. He notices many of the frozen items are damp from thawing, their conversation having gone on longer than he realized. Looking at some of the fruit that he just bought makes him hungry. Nolan grabs some cold leftovers from the fridge and sits down at the kitchen table to eat a bit before bed.

As he eats, Nolan thinks of Wyatt and the upcoming dinner they are going to have. Nolan tries to remember how long it's been since he did something like that. He couldn't. His wife was the one that always set up dinners and get togethers with friends. How much time had he spent alone in his chair because he was too content by himself?

That made him think of how his wife would have called him a 'head-strong idiot that didn't know any better' and then she would have hugged him and given him a kiss, saying that he was 'her headstrong idiot'. This made Nolan smile and happy for dinner on Thursday.

DISCLOSURE

Chapter 11

Rapid clicking of heels on wooden steps echoing through the stairwell. Dawn rarely takes these steps so fast, but she had so much fun at the club that she's still coming down from all the adrenaline. Finally, on the correct floor, she hums a bit of the last song from the dance floor while fumbling for her keys. Opening the apartment door, she finds the lights already on and one of her two roommates on the couch.

"Hey Jamie."

Looking up from her book she returns, "Oh, hey Dawn."

Dawn, still smiling, heads past the living room and towards the bedrooms. After entering hers, Dawn partially closes the door and quickly goes to sit down at her desk vanity. Once she collapses into her chair, Dawn leans back and sags her shoulders, letting her entire body relax and settle. But only for a few seconds. Once her body is entirely limp, her limbs move. Her feet kick off the heels that have been oppressing her all night while her hands remove her earrings.

Knocking on the bedroom door draws Dawn's attention, so she opens her eyes and looks over towards Jaime standing in the half-open doorway.

"You won't believe what my mom said to me today," she says

with a broad smile on her face.

Taking off the second earring, Dawn puts them away in her jewelry box and asks, "oh yeah, what did she say about me now?"

Jamie comes into the room and lays down on the bed. "Well she said the usual stuff, like how your lifestyle isn't something that God approves of."

"That sounds par for the course," Dawn says while wiping off her makeup.

"I know right? Anyway, she wanted to know when I was gonna find a new place to live."

"Don't we still have like a year on the lease?"

"Yep. But she even offered to pay the early cancellation fee if I moved out."

Finished removing her makeup, Dawn stands and takes off her dress to put on some sweatpants before realizing, "Wait... Wasn't that fee absurdly expensive? I remember we made fun of how bad it was."

"No. Yeah. I still think that part of the lease is illegal as shit."

Dawn takes off her bra and puts on a slightly baggy t-shirt. "So what did you tell her?", with a gleeful chuckle.

"Oh. I told her in no uncertain terms that I wasn't going to move anytime soon. Not unless she pays for my rent for the next three years."

Both of them laugh for a bit.

"How'd she take it?"

"Well she didn't like the idea of me hanging out with a guy that dresses like a girl, but overall, a lot better than I expected her to. I actually think she might be getting used to you living here. Plus, who can say that they know someone that can change from a woman into a man in under five minutes?"

Now sitting in front of the vanity mirror was Don, the man that had trouble interacting with people that weren't his friends, the man that spent most of his days working or staying at home. A man that felt more comfortable living as Dawn. But there he sat, looking at himself in the mirror, still happily riding the high of the club.

"I guess that is a very rare skill indeed. Maybe I should try out for the carnival."

"You seem happy! You never come back from the club this happy. What happened?"

Don thinks back on his night going out as Dawn. The lights and the music were oppressive as always, but not going out would have meant that they would have never met.

"I met a guy."

"Wait. Seriously? I've been trying to get you with my friend Matt for ages and now you find a guy in a club like a normal person?"

Don laughs a bit before answering. "He actually found me, we talked for a while and then he suggested that we dance for a bit."

"You? You danced?"

"Yep. You know how much I hate to dance, but doing it with him was so freeing. He made it so easy to open up and try new things."

Jamie moves around in a dancing motion and says in a sing-song voice, "Sounds like someone's got a crush..."

"Stop it." But Don knows that it's more than just a crush. But he also knows that he can't tell that to Jamie. He doesn't want to get ahead of himself. "Maybe just a little one."

"Just a little one? Your smile could light up half the block. Just a little one." Jamie lets out a stifled chortle.

"He… He made me feel beautiful. He made it feel like I was the only one in the room that mattered and that no one else's opinion in the club was important."

"Yeah. You need to be careful, you might get your heart broken if you're not."

"I know, it's just… It was such an amazing night. I haven't felt that way in a long time, and I don't think anyone's made me feel that good before."

Jamie gets up off of the bed. "I need to get to bed, and so do you."

"Okay, g'night."

"Night."

Jamie leaves and shuts the door; Don is left looking at himself in the mirror while applying his bedtime skincare routine. As he does, his mind once again goes back to thoughts of the club.

How it all started with Wyatt asking to drink together, Dawn had originally assumed that Wyatt was hitting on her, that made Dawn feel so pretty that she let her guard down. But after a bit, she realized Wyatt was a genuinely nice guy that just wanted a friend and thought that Dawn looked like a nice person. They had talked for so long about so many things that they eventually needed another round of drinks.

Wyatt had offered to get some fresh drinks and set off to the bar. No sooner than he was out of sight, a stranger approached the table. He had needed a place to sit for a while and asked if he 'could intrude for a few minutes'. Dawn's hackles rose. Was this some childish way to hit on her or try to 'steal' her away from Wyatt? But he didn't make a move; didn't even speak to her. He simply sat, biding his time until Wyatt returned with drinks in hand, and then introduced himself as if he'd been there the whole time. He explained that he had been dancing for the better part of an hour and just needed to sit down anywhere he could to get his breath back.

The three of them talked for an hour. They talked and asked questions of each other. Now and then, one of them would grab another round for the table. But after a while Wyatt had to bow out, he explained he wasn't used to drinking that much and that he needed to get home. Wyatt begrudgingly said his goodbyes and headed out.

That left Dawn with the charming newcomer. She knew by that time that she had more than just a simple crush on him. But over the next hour, they continued to talk about life and what their hopes and dreams were. Dawn felt like such a love struck school girl trying to find out anything and everything she could about this new infatuation. And by the end, Dawn realized that he seemed to be interested in her as well. She didn't know when it happened, but by the way he looked at her, how he touched her hand, or when they shared a laugh at a joke, it was different. At some point, they had moved closer; they started to always be in physical contact. They even danced for a bit, even though the thought of dancing in front of others terrified her. But in the end, they both knew that they needed to go home. Neither of them wanted to move too fast, they both wanted to leave on good terms. So they left the club together. And at the mouth of the alley, they went their separate ways.

Now ready for bed, Don gets under the sheets and turns out the lights. But as he drifts off to sleep, Don's thoughts keep going back to Seth and wondering when they would see each other next.

~TUESDAY~

SUNRISE

Chapter 12

The alarm clock went off, jolting Seth from sleep. It took what felt like a few minutes, but was most likely only a few seconds, to turn off the alarm. Laying in bed, Seth could feel the inside of his temples thump with the beat of a song from the club he was at the night before. Last night must have been crazy, because he could barely remember what happened.

Bits and pieces of the night flicker through his mind, pulsing with the beat of a phantom song trying to crack open his skull.

Seth pivots in bed to sit with his feet off the side and holds his hands over his eyes. Pushing his palms into his eyes, trying to rub at the itch that was an obviously terrible hangover. More parts of the previous night flicker, and he remembers the girl he met.

Wait.

What was her name?

Seth can only remember a bit about her. But flashes of dancing, talking well past midnight, and even the subtle scent of her perfume that he could just barely smell over the crowd in the club. As he remembers the subtle scent of lavender and vanilla, a bit of the euphoria of last night returns and some of the pain in his head subsides.

A wide grin of pleasure spreads on Seth's face.

Seth falls back onto the bed. Being with her last night made every night for the last few years seem dull in comparison. Seth raises his hand into the air and stretches it towards the ceiling. Reaching for something. Reaching for the memories of a woman that captivated him. Trying to grab hold of everything about her he could, and to grasp on so tight that it would never fade. With a clenched fist in the air, Seth closes his eyes and tries to remember her. He doesn't want to lose even a second of his fleeting memories from last night.

A rumble of a stomach makes Seth exhale in resignation. He needs food to get over the pain that is slowly crawling back into the foreground of his mind. He deliberately throws himself forward, gets up, and grabs some sweatpants before going to the kitchen.

On his way, he can see the first gleams of morning light coming through the large plate-glass windows in his living room. Some of the light reflects off of the sleek couches with tiny pillows that never get used. An interior designer placed them, claiming the layout 'really elevated the flow in the room' or some similarly worded nonsense. All he knew was that he pushed one of them 6 inches to the right after the fourth time he clipped his shin on a corner. The 'flow' didn't seem any different, but he never clipped his shin again.

Once in the kitchen, he instinctively grabs the large pan from the drying rack and puts it on the stovetop. After turning on the heat and putting a bit of oil in the pan, he opens the fridge to get two large sausages and two eggs.

Would she like it if I made her breakfast in the morning? Or would she want to make it for me instead?

Rolling the sausages in the pan while it heats, he cracks the eggs into a small bowl, adds some seasoning, and beats the eggs into a scramble with a little added milk. As the sausages heat a bit more, he grabs a glass for some orange juice.

While taking the orange juice from the refrigerator, Seth tries again to remember the name of the girl from last night. It's still sitting in the back of his head, but with such a splitting headache to deal with, he can't seem to remember.

Pouring the juice, he hoarsely says to himself, "I think... It started with a D."

Taking a sip of juice causes Seth to cough. The strong citrus attacks the back of his throat. It's a common issue for Seth. He loves orange juice, but on rare occasions he'll drink it in just the wrong way and the citrus will seem to adhere to the back of his throat.

As the sausages start to brown, he shakes the pan to roll them over to a new side. Standing there just looking at the pan, his mind wanders back. Her name had to start with a 'D'... It was something memorable, but not too unique either. Seth remembers how she shook her hips on the dance floor once she loosened up.

After a little more rolling and pan searing, Seth takes the sausages off the pan and puts them on the cutting board. Then pour the eggs into the pan. As they cook, he slices the sausages in half long-ways.

"Daisy... Diana... Doris! ...no." The returning headache forces him to stop guessing so he can think straight.

Once the eggs are almost done, Seth returns the sausages to the pan to brown the middles and slightly reheats them. After a bit, he scoops the food onto a plate and goes to sit down to eat at the breakfast bar.

As he eats he wishes that she had come home with him last night. Even if nothing happened, he could at least be talking to her right now instead of trying to puzzle out her name. Wait... Did he have her number!? He couldn't remember her giving it to him. But he does remember giving her his card before they split ways. What happens if she doesn't want to call? Should he try to find her? He can't do 'that' without knowing her name.

Taking a bite of his eggs, Seth feels defeated. It's not that the eggs are bad; they aren't. But it always seems like any time he gets eggs made for him, they are always fluffier and more flavorful than he can ever seem to make them. Taking a careful sip of the juice washes away some of the disappointment. But not all of it.

If I find her, what do I want? Do I want one night of passion? No. But... my life is on the road. Can I expect her to join me? Would she even want to? What kind of life would that be?

Seth goes back to eating his sad eggs and much tastier sausages. But in the back of Seth's mind, there's the knowledge of how he felt last night. Wishing that he would have remembered to get her number in the heat of the moment. Although, that would mean changing his entire outlook on going out like he has been. His standard operating procedure when out at a club is to never leave with anyone, never go out with anyone from work, and never stick with a group for more than two hours. In case sex is on the table, then he double checks consent for everything. Seth came up with this after having to sit in on way too many HR meetings surrounding inappropriate out of workplace incidents.

Would changing some things up be so bad?

No, but that also doesn't change the fact that I can't find her.

Done with his food, Seth puts the dishes in the dishwasher and heads back to the bedroom to get ready for work. As he gets ready for the day, Seth can't help but think of what little he can remember of the woman from the night before.

"I need to find this girl."

Looking at the clock, Seth realizes that he's running a little behind schedule and hurries up. On his way out of the apartment, he can see the rays of the sun finally cresting over the horizon. Seth stops for a second and relaxes.

"Dawn... Her name was Dawn."

A smile of absolute amusement spreads across Seth's face. He knows he won't be able to do anything productive until she calls.

"God, I hope she calls."

HARD DECISIONS

Chapter 13

Henry is enjoying his day-off sitting in the usual coffee shop just as he was the other day before talking with Seth. His wife has been under the assumption that for the past three months, Henry has been working six days a week due to staffing issues in his department because of the regional reorganization that's currently happening. Now, while the staffing issue is true, none of Henry's higher-ups have been willing to overwork him because of his normal throughput being so much above the others in his department. So, in reality, there have been weeks he's been given extra paid days off to make sure he doesn't leave the company. This is one of those days.

Normally, on one of these days, Henry would do everything in the morning like he was leaving for a normal day of work. He'd eat one of the excellent breakfasts his wife happily makes for him in the morning; and then he would come to this coffee shop for about an hour or two to read, decompress, and drink coffee. After that, he would spend the day with his mistress. This, however, is not a normal day off. Yesterday Henry decided that getting caught by Seth had to be the wake up call he needed. He was making his "work schedule" too busy; at some point, his wife might call his boss to complain and then find out just how many days off he had actually been getting recently. Then she would want to know what he was doing on all of those days off, and Henry wouldn't have a good enough answer. Not if he wanted to save his marriage.

So the plan for today was simple. He told his wife that he was coming down to the coffee shop for a bit and that he would be back later. She knows he loves coffee and enjoys time to himself, so she was happy enough to let him "Relax" on his day off. Then they planned to spend the day together. She was so happy to hear that Henry's boss gave him the day off that she started making plans for what they would do. Most of the time Henry would come to the shop and have a cup of coffee, or two, if he felt like he needed it that day, and then take a calming walk around the block before going off to whichever apartment he was going to that day. This, however, was a three cup day for Henry. It was such an unusual day that even the shop employees noticed the difference.

Don was cleaning up tables and trash around the shop when he noticed just how troubled Henry appeared to be. This didn't sit right with Don. Henry had been an amazing regular for so often that all the staff loved to see when he entered the shop. So, after taking a few seconds to muster up the courage to talk to Henry about what was bothering him, Don steps forward.

"Hey, Henry? Is everything alright?"

This startles Henry a bit and jogs him out of his thoughts. "Oh... No, uhh. I mean, yes. But, it's nothing you need to worry about."

"You sure? I have a minute if you want to talk about it."

"No... I'd hate to impose," Henry says, glancing down sheepishly.

"I insist," Don says, taking a seat next to Henry.

"I... I've realized that I've been doing a lot of things that I knew were wrong and that I should never have been doing. And yesterday I got called out for some of it. It made me realize how lucky I'd been to not be found out before this and how much worse it could have been."

"How bad are we talking here?"

"Well the small one is actually related to this shop. I've been taking my coffee breaks on company time and got caught."

"We were wondering how you got permission to take such long breaks in the middle of the day."

"Actually, my boss's boss said that I could continue to take my breaks as long as I clocked out and it didn't affect my work."

"Wait... Seriously?"

"No, yeah. He's been a great guy. It actually kind of makes me feel worse. I know that I messed up, and yet here I am getting away with cheating the company because the boss is a nice guy."

"Makes sense... But it also doesn't sound like the real issue."

It takes Henry a few seconds to work up the courage to say, "I... I've been seeing another woman behind my wife's back."

Both of them sit in silence. Don doesn't know how to respond to such an admission. Confessing to something like cheating on his wife wasn't something that Don was expecting to hear, and Don didn't know how he felt about Henry, now knowing what he knew. On the other hand, Henry felt that every second nothing was being said felt like a minute of torture.

To end the silence, Henry continued, "I know what I've been doing is terrible and that I never should have let something like this happen in the first place. But, it never felt like there was anything wrong. Until it was too late to stop it from happening in the first place, and then I didn't want it to stop."

Softly Don asks, "Do you ever plan on stopping?"

"I don't know. There have been plenty of times that I've left her apartment with the plan to never contact her again, and that I would block her from my phone. You know...? Clean start?"

"But... you never have?"

"Nope."

"Sooo. Why haven't you?"

With a bit of a laugh, Henry replies, "I'm not sure, but yesterday made me realize that I've been reckless."

"Now... I don't know the entire situation. But I've always believed that someone being reckless usually means they might want to be caught."

"Nooo," Henry says dismissively.

"Why not?"

Don picks up on the condescending tone while Henry replies, "Because I would never want to hurt my wife. She means too much to me."

Don takes a patient breath and deadpans, "So... why are you?"

Dumbstruck, Henry looks at Don with utter confusion.

Detecting Henry's hesitation, Don purses his lips before speaking. "Listen. You may not think that you want to cause your wife the pain of being cheated on, but you're still hurting her all the same. You may not want to admit it, but she isn't getting as much from you as she should."

Henry's eyes become downcast. He tried to muster up even a few syllables in his defence, but shame caught them in his throat.

Don continues, "Every time that you were with the other woman could have been time that you were spending with your wife. Every dollar you spent could have been spent on a gift for your wife. And every sexual thought that you had for your mistress could have been centered on your wife."

Henry continues to stay silent.

"Listen. Going out with another woman **will** hurt your relationship with your wife until she either finds out and is hurt, or **leaves** you because of neglect." After a few seconds Don continues, "I've had it happen to me before; it's never fun, and it always hurts."

"I know... I know you're right. But our relationship has been so strained and I just wanted to be happy."

"What do you mean by strained?"

After a quick exhale, Henry says, "I know it sounds bad and it feels like I only keep making it sound worse, but there are just so many issues that we fight about. Like how she keeps hounding me about my relationship with my son. At this point I just don't want to talk about it with her anymore."

"That may have been the reason you needed love and understanding, but that doesn't mean you should've sought that companionship with a new woman."

"You're right."

"Listen, I don't want to pry more than I already have. But what is so bad about your relationship with your son?"

"That's a whole other can of worms... We never seemed to understand each other. I love the boy with all my heart and would do whatever I could to make him happy. But I could never understand the things that he was into... One year, I got him a computer as a present, he must have sat in front of that thing for hours at a time. After a while I had no idea what he was doing on the thing. Now, every time he talks about computers, it just goes over my head and I have no idea what to say. And eventually, the only thing he wanted to talk about was computers. So we just kind of stopped talking all together."

"It sounds like you love him a lot." Don's warm smile returns.

"I do. But it's hard to find the words sometimes when I'm in front of him."

"Well you're better than some fathers."

Extremely confused, Henry looks over and asks, "What do you mean?"

"My father and I have always had a very... tumultuous... relationship to say the least, and down right hostile if I'm being honest. He never really respected my life choices."

"Now it's my turn to be sorry about prying, but what happened?"

"Well fair is fair... When my Dad found out about my 'lifestyle', it was my senior year of high school. We had a fight and he kicked me out of the house and told me in no uncertain terms to never come back or he would 'beat the queer' out of me."

Don looked up and was surprised to see Henry's face contorted in something close to pure anger. Don had never seen such a reaction from telling this story before. Most people would become sad or try to give him a hug in response to such a statement. And while there have been times that people have been mad at Don's father, the unbridled rage on Henry's face was new to Don. Seeing such a response actually made Don tear up a bit and place his hand on Henry's.

"Thank you." Don said.

"That's not a father," Henry replied coldly.

Holding back tears, Don softly asks, "What?"

"No father that loves their child could ever do that. I don't care what my son does with his life. I don't care if he becomes nothing and lives on the street. If he's happy and content, then I'm happy. I do want what's best for him, but... But what's best needs to be found out by him. Not whatever it is that I think is good for him."

"I mean it was a little bit my fault."

Henry looks Don straight in the eyes and asks, "Why? What gives your father the right to dictate how you'll live your life?"

"It was a small town and everyone was really religious. I knew growing up that I was different, and I also knew that I couldn't tell anyone. So... It was my fault for telling someone that I thought was a friend. By the end of the week, everyone in town knew."

"Have things gotten better since you moved to the city?"

"There are still people that look down on me like there's something wrong with me. But in the city it could just be a foul mouthed jerk that hates everybody."

"I guess that's an improvement." Henry shrugs.

"Yeah. Like there was this time about a year after I moved here that a guy on the first floor of my building kept calling me names and messing with my mail. I was so scared of him for so long. After he moved out, I was talking with some other tenants and found out that he did that to everyone."

"Equal opportunity bigot?" Henry cracks a shy grin.

"Basically," Don says with a laugh.

"How are you able to trust people after what happened?"

"Most of the time, people kind of figure it out before I have to tell them. But, I'm kind of selective when it comes to the people whose suspicions I'll confirm."

"Well... I'm honored to be one of the inner circle whose 'suspicions' have been confirmed." Henry stops with a look of surprised panic and looks at his watch. "Oh no, I need to get going. I'm supposed to do some shopping with my wife today."

"Well... let me get you a fresh cup for the road." Don said with a determined nod.

Both stand up from the soft chairs and walk up to the counter. Don walks around the side and pours some coffee into a to-go cup.

As Don is handing the coffee over, he says, "Take a few days to think things through. I know that you want to do what's right, but you don't want to make a snap decision that'll come back to bite you after the fact."

"Thanks for everything… And… I hope that the next person you find will appreciate both sides of you."

With a smile and the hint of a laugh, "Me too."

Henry leaves the shop with more to think about than when he came in, but less confused about what he would do in the end.

Don gets back to work cleaning up the sitting area of the shop. While organizing a pile of newspapers, he thinks about what Henry said to him before he left.

"Both sides… Oh no." It echoes in his head as he stops moving in the middle of the shop.

Dread grips onto Don and refuses to let go. With all the joy he had been feeling regarding Seth, he hadn't considered that Seth didn't, couldn't, have known his secret yet. Seth was so nice and such a normal well put-together person, there's no way that someone like him would understand or be in love with someone like Don if he knew the truth.

Under his breath, Don lets out a barely audible, "Fuck… What am I going to do now?"

Slowly, Don sits down in a chair and looks blankly out of the storefront window. With his mind racing a mile a minute, he tries to think of a way to proceed. But nothing he can think of gets past the point where he has to tell Seth the truth.

WELCOME HEALING

Chapter 14

Wyatt wakes to his usually dark room in a happier manner than he has in years. Even Though he's still a bit physically exhausted from the night before, his mind feels refreshed and invigorated. Rolling over in bed, he sees the lights of his computer casting a monotone glow that never shuts off. Taking his time, Wyatt stretches his body and flexes his muscles in pleasure. Eventually, he decides that he's rested enough and begins getting out of bed.

Once standing, Wyatt doesn't know what to do. If this was a usual day, he would sit down at his computer; but the previous night's fun has him rethinking. There he stands, behind his computer chair, wondering if he actually wants to sit down. Wyatt knows that if he does, the rest of the day will be set in stone. As he stands there waiting and thinking of the possible repercussions that would come from sitting in his own chair, his stomach growls. A particularly large growl that seemed to come out of nowhere, causing Wyatt to laugh, so he chooses food instead of sitting.

In the kitchen, Wyatt searches his cabinets for food. Fresh ingredients are scarce, but he finds enough for a bowl of cereal. Still not wanting to sit down, even if it's at the kitchen table, Wyatt wanders around his apartment while eating his bowl of cereal. As he walks, he realizes just how dark and dirty his apartment has become.

Wyatt makes his choice. He doesn't want to live like this.

The joy and freedom of last night still plays in his mind. He wants to live life to its fullest. He wants to work, not just for the time to play a game in what little off time there is. He wants to explore and find joy with friends that he can touch or talk face-to-face with. He wants to live.

After finishing breakfast, Wyatt looks at the dishes in the sink. The clutter on the counters and the general mess of the apartment gives him a shudder. He decides to clean. Looking at his clock, Wyatt decides he will go out for lunch as a reward if he can clean the apartment until 11:00. With that much time, he should be able to make a dent in the major cleanliness issues of the apartment.

Getting out some large black trash bags, Wyatt starts by going around each room and collecting up the obvious trash. Empty soda cans and pizza boxes almost fill up two full trash bags by themselves. Loose paper and junk mail that clutter up the corners of the counter get tossed. Amazon boxes from months ago that were never flattened or thrown away finally stop cluttering up the living room. To top off the bag, Wyatt takes down the cardboard and tape covering the windows. With fresh morning light coming through the windows for the first time in years, Wyatt's smile widens, and he places the full trash bags by the front door.

Wyatt takes a second to look at his apartment. There aren't any more piles of garbage cluttering the rooms, but there are still tons of tiny knick-knacks filling up spaces. Most were purchased because of a passing fancy, or an in-the-moment love of a character or series. But now, most of the love has gone stale. Most of the memories are hazy half-remembered jokes or triumphs that weren't even his own. So Wyatt grabs another bag and starts filling it up with any knick-knack that he doesn't have an immediately positive memory of. This actually leaves him with more space to showcase his now prominent items that have larger sentimental value to Wyatt as a whole.

With all three bags filled, the apartment feels less like a cave and more like a home. After throwing out the garbage bags, he comes back to the clock saying 10:04.

So the next step is dishes. Hot soapy water and mindless scrubbing consumes his subconscious. Plates find their way into the dishwater. Such a task leaves little but for the mind to wander. Wyatt thinks about Nolan and what they are going to eat later in the week. It's been years since he actually sat down and ate with someone in person. To believe that such a thing could mean so much now. This makes Wyatt wonder what other things in his life seemed boring at first and so took them for granted.

As Wyatt leaves the last of the pots to dry in the rack, the clock shows 10:26. So Wyatt grabs some paper towels and a bottle of knock-off window cleaner. He starts with the windows and plans to clean the bathroom mirror next. Just another repetitive task, but oddly calming. Something that's easy to accomplish but has a definitive and visible rate of progress.

Wyatt thinks back on what Nolan had said the night before, about his father. "Maybe I do need to take the first step." Wyatt looks around to find an apartment that looks nothing like the one that he's lived in for the last few years. If he didn't clean it himself, Wyatt would have assumed that he was in the wrong apartment.

The clock says 10:38 and Wyatt decides that this is good enough for now. Decompressing from cleaning, he feels it's a good time for lunch. He thinks about the laughable breakfast he's already had this morning and wonders if somewhere is still serving breakfast. Or brunch... He could always get a waffle and sausage at some place that does brunch. His mother always loved brunch, she would have them go out for brunch every few months. Everyone seemed to enjoy such an easy outing together.

"Hmmm. Why not ask them out for brunch?" he wonders aloud.

Wyatt decides he should take the first step. Calling them up, he gets their voicemail.

"Hey Mom, Dad…it's Wyatt. I was just calling because I was wondering if you guys wanted to go to brunch with me this weekend. I don't know if you're busy, but I was thinking maybe next Sunday. Give me a call if you want to go. Love you guys, bye."

Wyatt hangs up with a smile, knowing that he did the right thing. Looking around his apartment, Wyatt decides he should buy a vacuum… and a mop. He's never needed to vacuum or mop before, because the room was never clean enough to see the floor or all of the dirt caked onto it before.

"Welp time for lunch."

Wyatt leaves the apartment with a wide grin on his face. Once on the street, he starts walking to a restaurant two blocks away.

Wyatt never makes it to the restaurant.

While crossing the street, a taxi driver falls asleep at the wheel.

Three people are run over before the taxi crashes into another car.

Wyatt dies before the ambulance is called.

Seven minutes later, Henry and his wife walk through their front door. They're returning from a quick shopping trip and a stop by a nearby restaurant with some takeout. Henry goes to the kitchen to unpack the bag with their food when he sees the flashing light of the answering machine.

Henry presses the play button and listens to Wyatt's message while he finishes taking out the food. Happy to hear from his son, he goes to tell his wife about the message and to ask if they already have plans for Sunday. Just as excited to see Wyatt as Henry is, she double checks their schedule to make sure. She has Henry call Wyatt back to set up a time while she plates the food for them both.

Henry's message is as follows, "Hello, son. It's great to hear from you. Your mother and I would love to get some brunch this Sunday. Let's get in touch tonight to set up the time and place. Talk to you soon. Love you. Bye."

As Henry hangs up the phone, he can't help but smile.

Both of them sit down to eat. Neither of them know that this will be the last meal from this restaurant that won't remind them of their son's death.

~FRIDAY~

DROWNING NECTAR

Chapter 15

Despair and stale beer permeate the bar. No one usually comes to this establishment in the daytime unless they have a specific sorrow that they want to drown. Don finds himself frequenting this bar the past few days specifically to do just that.

Don still worries about what he should do about Seth. He knows that there should be no way that Seth knows his secret. But he also knows that he wants to be with Seth, that he hasn't felt this kind of 'puppy love' in a long time. So... he drinks. Don drinks away the feelings of love and dread. He drinks until his body becomes numb to the world around him and he can finally have peace from his own emotions. A small part. A very tiny part is also trying to find courage at the bottom of each bottle that's finished. The courage to embrace the pain and to find Seth; to tell him the truth and to believe in the fairytale of love.

"It's all bullshit."

Nolan walks in the bar and sees that one of the men is much younger than the usual crowd. He can also tell that the pain this man feels is fresher than the others. Everyone else in the bar has had to live with the demons that brought them to this bar for a very long time, and he hates to see someone wallow with fresh demons alone.

So Nolan moves to a seat beside Don and asks, "Is this seat

free?"

Looking up with barely a hint of being drunk, Don curtly says, "No."

Nolan sits down anyway and waves to the bartender. "I find it's never a good idea to drink alone."

"What'll you have, sir?", asks the bartender.

"Scotch. Anything over 18 years... Neat." Nolan says while looking expectantly to the selection behind the bar.

With a smile the bartender replies, "Right away, sir," turns and walks towards the bottles on the wall.

Don sits in his chair drowning his sorrows.

"You know. I never really liked Scotch... Not at first at least. It took me a while to develop the taste and to get used to drinking harder liquor." Nolan explains while never taking his eyes off the bottles behind the bar.

"Oh yeah?" Don replies in a monotone.

"Yep... I liked the idea of Scotch... I must have forced myself to drink the stuff for years before I figured it out."

Nolan looks over to Don, an almost empty beer in his hand and a soft worry behind his eyes. The bartender returns with a glass. Nolan gives him a credit card and asks to open a tab.

After the bartender walks away, Nolan continues, "I tried a lot of different types and varieties. And I couldn't tell you how many years it took, but I found what works for me."

"I've never touched the stuff," Don coldly retorts.

"Oh yeah? I always find there's a story behind words like those," Nolan seems amused.

"My dad drank Scotch. Never... Seemed appealing after that." Don turned away slightly.

"Not a good father?"

Don turns back again and says, "he used to tell me all the time that all things worth something required time... But he was never willing to put in the time himself... He would save up enough money to buy an old beater of a car with plans of repairing and flipping it for a ton of money. Then he would sell it for enough money to buy more Scotch a month later."

They both find themselves sitting in silence with their drinks.

Grumpilly Don finally asks, "So what brings ya in here?"

With a gentle sigh, Nolan replies, "I'm going to a funeral tomorrow." Both of them sit as the words seem to stretch time. "He was young. Too young. But he lived down the hall from me. We'd never talked, except for the night before he died. The poor boy was so nice, it felt like he was finally coming into his own."

"I'm sorry for your loss." Don says, loosening up slightly.

"I'm used to burying friends... But usually the people that I have to see buried aren't so young."

They share another respectful silence as they both sip their drinks.

Nolan looks over to Don and pointedly asks, "I hate to be so forward, but what's causing you such an obvious pain?"

Don puts on a fake smile and looks over to Nolan and asks, "what makes you think I'm in pain?"

"I've seen enough friends try to drown their sorrows over the years to know what it looks like... Hell. I've seen it in the mirror enough times after my wife died. You aren't fooling anyone. Not in this bar."

The two lock eyes for a few seconds before Don's eyes fall and he responds, "I found someone that I really like... Someone that I think I'm in love with."

"Okay? That doesn't explain the sadness. But I get the

feeling that that's not the end of the story." Nolan lets out a wise sigh.

"Nope... Our 'relationship' was based on a lie. Quite a big lie at that... Now I don't think I can come clean without losing the relationship, and if I try to fool him, then Seth will definitely find out, and I don't know if he'll love me afterwards."

Nolan stops for a second and looks at Don. "Wait a minute, hold up."

Don freezes. He realizes he let it slip out. Questions of whether this older man approves of two men being together rush through his mind. He's scared that the only nice person he's met all day will turn on him in a second because of his sexuality. Don waits for the oncoming tirade that he expects to be flung his way.

"You just said love for the second time."

Don unclenches a little in surprise.

"Not 'like' or 'interested in'... You said love... And love is always something worth fighting for."

Don's heart beats faster. He can feel the tears well in the corners of his eyes.

Nolan urges, "if you want to find love, you have to be prepared to let them know all of your secrets. Because that's what mutual love means you can do without fear of hatred or reprisal."

Both men sit in silence for a while, letting the words sink in as they drink.

"But then again, you should never make any sort of decision while you're drunk. Unless that is, the decision to become less drunk." Nolan leans in closer to Don and whispers, "it never turns out well otherwise."

Don hesitates and chuckles, "No... You're right."

Nolan clicks his tongue. "I don't want to be rude... but... so far, what you've told me isn't that bad. You fell for someone that doesn't know your secret, and it would suck if they found out. So what am I missing?"

Don wonders if he should tell the truth to this man that he only met a few minutes ago. He has been nothing but cordial and considerate to Don, but talking about his past isn't the easiest thing to do.

Nolan sees the hesitation and says, "come on, you're alive and healthy looking. So while it might be bad, it shouldn't be so bad you can't talk about it."

Don nervously responds, "I live two different lives. One of them is the person you see before you. This is the person that gets up in the morning and goes to work to make money, or the person that goes out for a drink when it's the middle of the day." A little more quietly, Don continues, "but when I can safely be myself, I am a woman named Dawn. And the night that I met Seth, I was out at a club as her."

"Ahhh. I see... That could be a problem, but it's not insurmountable. But that still doesn't answer my question." Nolan says in a soft and supportive tone.

"You know the little that I've told you about my father. Well it was hell living with him. It was rare... But he had the potential to be a violent drunk. I grew up knowing only to fear him. But in my last year of Highschool, he and the whole town found out about my secret. So when I got home and found him angry drunk, I knew that I was in trouble. He beat me, on and off for the better part of an hour and then tossed me outside in the dark. He told me that if I wasn't gone by the morning, he would 'beat the queer out of me before shooting me where I stood'."

Nolan could feel the pit of his stomach drop out from under him and get replaced with an anger that he could rarely remember feeling. "I'm guessing nothing happened to him."

Don studies Nolan's face. "It's funny... Before this week, I can't remember seeing the kind of fire that's in your eyes after telling this story. But now I've seen it twice in a few days."

Coldly, Nolan responds, "It's the rage of a father."

"What?" Don was taken aback.

"This... is the rage of a father that knows the joys and pains of raising a child. And the utter contempt for the kind of man that could have a child and then treat them in the way you've described. As a man... I know the depravity of this world is beyond what most are willing to know. But I can't stand the knowledge that someone chose to treat their child in such a manner."

Don's eyes glistened. "Thank you, but it's all in the past. And hate is still the kind of reaction I've learned to expect over the years."

"I understand, I would help if I could." Nolan noticeably relaxes a little.

"It's fine, the pain isn't as sharp as it used to be." Don stands up and asks the bartender for the check. As he pays, he looks to Nolan and says, "I'm sorry for your loss... And... thanks for the advice."

"When you're my age, you realize that giving advice is just about the only thing you can do to help people anymore." Nolan raises his glass at something nobody else can see.

Don walks away, returns, and then tells the bartender, "I'm buying my friend here another round." Opens his wallet and puts a twenty-dollar bill on the counter. Don waves goodbye and heads out of the bar with a sway in his step.

As Don leaves the bar, the bartender picks up the money and says, "Hey... Your new friend left a business card with the twenty." After an awkward pause, he looks directly at Nolan and says, "You know that a twenty won't cover you for a second."

Nolan laughs a bit and nods his head. "No, I know. How 'bout you give me the business card and you can keep the money as a tip."

The bartender brightens up, winks, and hands over the card without complaint. Nolan sees the name Seth on the card. He thinks about it for a second and puts the card into his pocket.

LOST DIVINITY

Chapter 16

Don is walking down the sidewalk with little to no idea of where he's heading. All he knows is that the buzz of alcohol is making his mind sluggish and fuzzy. What little extra mental capacity he has after making himself walk down the street is being spent on thinking about the really nice old man from the bar. That's when Don realizes that he never got the old man's name.

"Well, I'll ask him if we ever see each other again," he says under his breath.

Don continues to think about the old man and how he wished he could have been his father instead of the one he had. As he wanders the streets, Don gradually feels more and more intoxicated. Slowly, his mind wanders to the sidewalk itself and Don becomes lost in the rhythm of his steps and the spacing of the lines of the sidewalk. Eventually, the lines and his steps sync up, causing him to hyper focus on the ground instead of what's happening around him.

Passing by an alleyway breaks the rhythm and jostles Don's mind free from the clutches of drunken tunnel vision. That's when he becomes hyper fixated on what he must look like to everyone around him. How odd he must look staring at the ground and almost stumbling through the city. Deciding to blend into those around him better, Don raises his head to look straight ahead and actively tries to walk in a straight and deliberate fashion.

This actually seemed to work well for a block or two, with Don being able to stay in the flow of sidewalk traffic fairly easily. But after a bit, he thinks of how beautiful large masses of people walking down the street must appear when looked at from above. Each person changes their paths in order not to touch or interact with one another while getting to their destination as fast as possible. How a single slow person can act like a rock in the river of traffic, causing eddies of turbulence in the overall flow of people.

This new line of thinking seems to hit Don all at once and eventually made his mind try to visualize the street he was currently walking down from an aerial perspective. Doing that made Don's head spin wildly to the point of needing to stop. It feels as if the world wouldn't allow Don to continue, so he stumbled his way over to the nearest doorway. Bent over with his hand on the wall, he watches all the passersby that keep trying to secretly take a glance his way without looking at him directly. Each person is in their own world with their own lives and problems, but each one of them is actively trying to look into Don's world without actually taking the time to enter it. They want to be the fly on the wall without actually being a part of the situation itself. None of them seem to care that another human is in obvious pain and in need of compassion. Even though they're within a hand's reach; they would sooner take out their phones and take a video of the situation before actually trying to help the person in need. Don feels an overwhelming sense of loneliness, but as his stomach sinks in despair, he feels a hand on his shoulder.

Luke was walking along the street when he saw a man struggling in the doorway of a building. Most people would see a homeless man, someone mentally ill, or a drugged-up person to be avoided at all costs. But to Luke, he knows the signs of each of those things from working weekends at shelters and soup kitchens. He knows from the signs that this man is drunk, but that this is a recent issue, and not something that he's had to live with for a long time. So Luke wants to give the man a helping hand.

Luke puts his hand on the other man's shoulder and says, "Looks like you could use some help."

"Oh. no... I'm just not feeling that well."

"Well... My name's Luke, what's yours?"

Don is a bit taken back. He was expecting this random stranger to, at most, see if there was an issue and then ask him to leave. Instead, this man, Luke, seems to be genuinely worried about Don's safety. It doesn't seem like he's about to scream, fight, or call the cops on Don. So, reluctantly, he answers, "My name's Don."

"Well Don, it's great to meet you. But I still can't help but think that you're in need of help. So... I'll ask again. Do you need anything?" Luke's determination blazes on his face.

"I'm a bit beyond help at this point."

"Now that is something I'm gonna have to refute. No one's beyond help, except for those that won't accept it."

With a bit of a laugh, Don replies, "Then I guess I must be unwilling."

Don looks up to see Luke's face spread out in a smile.

"That may be... But that doesn't mean I'm gonna stop trying."

"Listen, I... Thanks, but I should go... I need to go." Don tries to take a few steps into the flow of foot traffic. His head spins from the sudden movement and then leans back into the wall of the building.

"Woah, woah, woah. Careful there. I've got you," Luke says as he helps steady Don from falling down.

"No. You shouldn't be helping me. I'm not worth it."

Luke sees the dejection on Don's face, the self hatred overwriting the embarrassment of saying such a thing out loud. "How about this, I'll help you for a few blocks so that you can get your feet under you. I'm going in that direction anyway."

"I never said where I was going."

"Neither did I." A half grin sneaking onto Luke's face.

Don can't help but laugh at the absurdity of the situation. He can't think of anyone that's acted like this in their everyday lives. Hell, even the old man from the bar was there to drink. But this man was 'out of the goodness of his own heart', stopping to make sure that Don was okay and taken care of.

Gesturing down the street, Don says, "I guess a little help from strangers never helped."

As they start moving, Luke chuckles, "I think you said that wrong."

"Oh? Did I? Must have been a Freudian slip."

"A what?" Luke cocks his head to the side slightly while still walking.

"It means that I said what I really thought on accident. Drunk sincerity?" Don, sobering up slightly, hears what he says and looks down.

Don stumbles a bit, but Luke quickly steadies him before they continue walking.

Luke continues, "That seems really pessimistic."

"How is mixing my words up pessi... Pessa... Pessimistic...?" Don looks to Luke, slightly affronted, then shakes his head and resumes walking.

"No." Luke laughs, "The words you mixed up."

"Oh." Chuckling as well, Don admits, "Yeah, I guess that

does make more sense now that you say it."

They both walk in silence with a few lingering giggles between the two of them. As the silence continues, Don gets serious.

Looking over, Don asks, "Why did you stop?"

Gesturing with his head behind them, Luke asks, "Back there?"

"Yeah... Why did **YOU**, out of all the others passing by on the street. Why did **YOU** stop?" Don pauses to stable himself.

Luke gets serious as he thinks before letting out a big exhale and asks, "have you read the bible?"

A bit surprised, Don returns, "I mean... My parents had me go to Sunday school... But I can't really quote you any verses."

"Well... Do you remember Mathew 25?"

"Noooo... Can't say that I do. Now it might just be the absurd amount of alcohol flowing through my veins... But I'm pretty sure that I have no idea what that one says."

"Well..." Luke smiles, "At the end of Mathew 25, God tells those that have been good to others and helped those in need that they will stay by his side."

With a bit of excitement, Don says, "Oh oh wait. Was that the whole people are sheep and goats. For I was hungry and thirsty so you gave me some stuff to eat and drink?"

Sharing in the excitement, Luke returns, "Yeah! That's the one. I mean... Not word for word... I'm not sure if there's a lot of people saying 'so you gave me some stuff' in the bible. But, that's the one."

"Well now who's being all pessimistic?" Don starts off with a confident strut.

Luke has to speed up a little to keep up before they sync up again. "How so?"

"Well... You're saying that the only reason you're helping me out is because either you do or God will punish you. Doesn't that seem a little pessimistic about God and how he acts? I mean, he's supposed to be all knowing, all powerful, and yet you think he's gonna punish you for not helping someone when they need help but will reward you for helping if your intentions are to just not get in trouble." Don wears a confident smile.

Luke tilts his eyes up thoughtfully. "It's not really that literal."

"It's like a cop arresting a person for obstruction when his family is being threatened by a gang the cops are looking into. And then the cops let one of the gang members off of a murder charge when he gives up a few other gang members. It seems black and white on the face, but when you look deeper, it's all mostly gray."

Luke has a long contemplative blink. "I think I understood like half of that."

Realizing how he's coming across, Don sullenly replies, "listen... You seem like a great guy. I just have my own issues."

They both get quiet for a few seconds and let their conversation marinate in their minds.

Luke breaks the silence with, "You know. I've been having trouble lately."

With genuine concern in his voice, Don replies, "With what?"

"Every time I go to church, I wonder why... I feel lost in the sea of those that believe... even though I'm physically there more than any of them." Luke says while fidgeting with his hands.

"Isn't that what church is for?" reassures Don non-sarcastically.

A look runs across Luke's face. "Okay?...How so?"

"Those that are lost are the ones that need the church the most. Even when they're lost in the church."

"I guess that makes a sort of sense." Luke's eyes warm but he still faces forward.

As they walk for a bit, Luke can tell that Don has something on his mind but waits for him to come to his own decision.

Slowly Don explains, "Listen... I had a hard time leaving my town when I moved here. Not because everyone was sad... or that I missed everyone. I was basically exiled. All of my friends and family wanted me gone. And mostly because of what most would consider 'religious' reasons."

Luke stops dead. It took Don half a step to realize that he hadn't slowed, but had stopped completely. Don looks at Luke while he's paralyzed in thought.

"The whole town? That's... That's horrible."

With a grimace, Don explains, "I know. But... That's why I'm so negative towards religion in general. So make sure to take any of my advice on the subject with a grain a salt."

"I'm so sorry you had to deal with such a... terrible side of religion like that. I've always seen religion as a way to better myself. As a way to help all of mankind better themselves... So I've always tried to live my principles. That way others can see, and take them into their own lives."

Don considers hopefully, "Does that work?"

"Not all the time. In fact, I just got reprimanded at work. Apparently people thought I was 'going too far' and 'pushing God' onto them."

"I don't know you all that well, but I think you might be trying to 'share' your religion because you're not so sure of it right now either." Don attempts straightening up, only to immediately slouch back down again.

They walk in silence, processing what's been said. As they pass a shop window, Don catches something in his eye and realizes where they are, head swimming.

"Oh... That's my building. I'll... I'll manage from here."

They look at each other. Both having shared such a strange conversation that neither will forget it for a long time. Both sorry to see the other go.

Luke breaks the silence with, "Make sure you take care of yourself."

"I will. And thanks for the help."

Luke waits for a few seconds and then says, "Don. I'm... I'm sorry you had such a hard time in your hometown."

"Thanks Luke. I have a feeling that if you were there when I was younger it wouldn't have been so bad."

Luke feels better about himself and smiles. They leave each other, both happier with the world than when they met. Though they both still carry holes in their hearts, they've each helped in healing the other's wounds.

~SATURDAY~

LAMENTING HEAVEN

Chapter 17

Darkness.

Soft breaths that rush as loud as a river in the mind.

It's been days of endless wandering. Searching for anything to end the pain. Anything that could make it even slightly tolerable.

Henry wonders why he thought this place would help. Tall ceilings with large panes of glass letting in light, wooden pews for worship, or the promise of salvation from one's troubles.

It was probably the last one.

Probably the need to end the suffering.

The need to end anything and everything.

To just. Stop. The pain.

In truth, Henry really doesn't remember exactly how he ended up in such a place. It had been happening a lot since he found out on Tuesday. He would decide that he needed to move. That sitting still was almost painful. That seeing his wife was painful, not because of anything she did, but because of the pain that they shared. Because he couldn't sit next to someone feeling the same things that he was currently feeling and not weep for her pain. The pain was less when he was elsewhere. So he moved. He rarely stopped, because stopping allowed him to think. Stopping brought him back to the pain.

On Thursday, his wife had joined him for most of the day. Trying to help bridge the gap between their pains. To help Henry heal enough to return to her in full. It didn't help. She knew he needed time, and that she could at least give him that. So now she waits for him to come home in the evenings, with a hot meal, a clean house, a warm shower, and a comfy bed. She used the time he was gone to plan the funeral.

Henry's not ready to think about funerals.

But Henry also realizes that he's not alone. He looks around, hoping to find the one person who he wishes to see most in this world. But Wyatt isn't there. Instead, Henry sees a man sitting two pews behind him.

"When did you get here?" asks Henry.

"I've been here for a while. Recently it seems like I'm always here."

Both of the men sit in silence; neither one judging the other for their words, each just trying to figure out what to do next.

In resignation, Henry looks towards the altar and speaks, "Why?... Why is God such an asshole?"

Unphased by Henry's declaration, he stands up and, with purpose, walks up the pews to sit down next to Henry. Nothing in the man's posture shows malice or hatred for the words he just uttered. Instead, Henry finds the face of someone worried. Worried not for the wrath of God or humans for speaking ill of a vengeful God within his place of worship, but instead, worried for the pain that made speaking such words possible.

"Sounds like you need to talk to someone other than God for a while."

With derision laced in his voice, Henry sobs, "God... Why? Why does his words seem so empty in times of real need for comfort?"

"It's because his are the kinds of words that we want to hear."

"You saying I don't want to feel better?"

"Well? Do you?"

They both sit in silence, neither knowing what to add.

Henry changes the subject by asking, "You said you've been spending a lot of time here recently."

With understanding, the man smiles a bit and looks towards the altar, "I've had my own personal issues with God as of late. When I was a kid, God used to be this omnipotent power that was larger than everything. He was able to help his believers and punish the sinners. He made the world a better place. But as I grew up... I realized that there were bad people that were never punished by either God or humans. I realized that good people died well before their time, and that sometimes the worst of us outlive Saints... But. I still chose to believe. I held out hope for a better future, and I held onto the faith that God knows what needs to be done."

"But what does that have to do with spending more time in church?"

"As I'd grown and the magic faded away, I've tried to get the feeling back by giving myself over to God, by coming to pray more and more often. I come to church to feel like how it used to be. To pray for that feeling of right and wrong. For the feeling that evil will be punished and that God loves us all. I guess I thought that coming to church more often would make it more likely that God would bless me with a sign or at least something to help me find my way."

"I guess from the way you're talking, it hasn't really helped."

"No... Not in the long run. If anything I'm starting to feel more and more drained, the faith that I used to feel has dried up, and I feel left behind... And in the end, I seem to be on the verge of losing my job because of it."

"That's not good... I had something similar happen a few days ago. I was taking advantage of my position in the company and taking breaks that I shouldn't have. The big boss called me out on it, but gave me another chance. I'm thankful for that chance. But... It makes me wonder why he gave it to me. What did he see in me that told him to give me that chance?"

"I know it's kind of odd and a bit of a non-sequitur, but you talking about that makes me think of something that happened yesterday. I was on my way home and found a man on the street. He was obviously drunk and needed some help, and like most people, I would have usually walked around him and tried not to interact or get pulled in. But... then I saw something."

After the pause becomes so long that Henry can't stand not to know, he asks, "What did you see?"

"Oh... I saw that he was in pain. Not just a normal pain. The same kind that I've been going through with the church. A pain of the soul... I saw a bit of myself in that man. But I knew in that moment that I needed to help, that I would do whatever I could to help heal that man's pain. I know it sounds cheesy, but that's how it felt."

Henry, with a flat voice, says, "It sounds like you mean it."

Both sit in silence. They let the echoes of the room surround themselves.

"My son died on Tuesday."

Everything made sense now. The anger, the pain, the yearning for answers that can never be found.

"I'm sorry. I wish there was something, anything, that I could do to help. But I know that even me telling you that can only do so much."

"Each day has been its own little hell. Each day I wake up in ignorance until I'm reminded of the pain. And I don't know what's worse. The fact that the pain won't go away, or the knowledge that some day it'll fade. That some day, the pain that I feel for losing my son will diminish. That I'll become used to knowing he's dead. That I'll stop grieving his absence."

"I don't know your pain. But I can stay with you as long as you would like."

Keeping back a sob, Henry thinks of something and says, "I know this may sound odd. But I have something to ask of you."

"What can I do to help?"

"Today is the service. My wife's spent the last few days putting it all together, and I know that I should have been there already. And it's nothing big or flashy... But, that's part of the problem. We couldn't find many of his friends. There were some people that knew of him, but most had never talked with him before... I know that it's last minute. But it would really help to know that there were more people there for my boy's funeral."

Understanding the issue, he replies immediately, "I would be honored to be there for you and your son."

"Thank you so much. It means so much, mister... you know. I don't know your name."

"It's Luke, but that's not important right now."

As they both stand to go, Henry continues to hold back tears. He knows that if he started crying, he wouldn't be able to stop for some time.

Luke leads Henry down the aisle and out of the church, while asking what his name is in turn.

Now silent and empty, the church shows no sign of the kinds of emotions that just filled the room. Instead, the lights still shine through the glass and silence purifies the space.

AN HONEST NARRATOR

Chapter 18

Nolan stands off by himself in the back of the much too large room. White folding chairs have been lined up in rows, too many seats, and not enough people. But at the front lies the monolith, the tomb of cedar and brass. Such a tableau has started wars, made men cry, and has Nolan locked in place unable to look up or talk for the last twenty minutes.

Nolan keeps going over the first, last, and now only time that he and Wyatt spoke. Their talk of Wyatt's relationship with his father and how rocky the relationship was seemed so innocent at the time, but now it feels like an invasion. A settling unease that seems to spread though Nolan's body, then gradually recedes before he remembers just where he is, causing the feeling to spread again.

Nolan and his wife worked hard to have a wonderful life with his family and the grandchildren that they could watch grow. And for a very long time, they were able to enjoy all of it. But this... this is such perfect proof that joy could be ripped out from under you at a moment's notice. What would he do if the life they built was destroyed before Nolan dies? His children have grown and become wonderful parents, but what if it was one of his grandchildren instead of Wyatt?

No.

You mustn't think like that.

Such thoughts lead down a dark path. Taking such a path is a recipe for emotional pain and torture. His family is safe, and that's how he has to remember them.

But what if they're taken? The pain of the question hits Nolan like a physical force, blanking his mind before he can forcefully clear it once more.

As his mind clears, Nolan can hear people walking in the hallway, causing him to look towards the newcomers. The sounds of the two men that enter have drawn the attention of the entire room, the noticeable lack of mourners making it easier. An older gentleman is flanked by a younger one who doesn't look around for anyone he might know. Instead, he waits by the older man's side and moves with him at a respectful distance. Both move towards Wyatt's mother, who is standing near the memory table. As they reach Wyatt's mother, she talks with the older man while looking quite peeved. After a bit of talking, she looks past the older man and with a smile introduces herself to the younger one. He returns her somber smile and offers his hand to shake. The three of them talk for a bit before she steps aside to show the younger man the items on the memory table.

The younger man's entire demeanor freezes up. His face goes a bit pale and Nolan has a sinking feeling the young man is about to pass out. But before Nolan could do anything, he stumbles forward a bit and picks up a framed picture of Wyatt. Wyatt's mother and the older man seem worried and gesture to sit down. The older man rushes over to the nearest folding chain and brings it over for the young man.

As he's made to sit in the chair, all that Nolan can make out is, "but... I met him... earlier this week."

Hearing that forces Nolan's eyes down again. As the realization of what he had just seen sinks in. Nolan's mind goes blank. He was never one to keep himself from crying, but he tends not to cry in front of others. It's never been an issue of bravado or machismo. Instead, it was because Nolan saw crying as a deep and personal matter. So being in a situation where water was now welling up in his left eye was a surprise even to himself. Not wanting to hold in such emotions, he chose to embrace the pain. He took some deeper breaths to steady himself and let the pain wash over this moment in his mind. Closing his eyes and taking in a deep breath, Nolan lifts his head towards the light. After a few more breaths, the tear rolls off his cheek. His steady breathing slowly brings a calm over Nolan's emotions. With the rushing onslaught dying down, the remaining sadness could be felt and processed.

"Sir?"

Startled, Nolan's eyes jump instead of his body. As his eyes flutter open, Nolan sees the older of the two men in front of him. He sees Wyatt's mother comforting the younger man that is now sitting in a folding chair dealing with his own emotions. Focusing back onto the older man, Nolan, with the faintest of cracks in his voice, says, "I... I'm sorry, hello."

"My wife's told me that you knew my son, so I just wanted to thank you for coming."

"Oh, yes... He," choking up a bit at the thought of Wyatt, "was a good man."

The man that Nolan now assumed was Wyatt's father smiled a bit at that. "Thanks for your kind words. I only wish that I knew him better as the man he had become."

With trepidation, Nolan wonders if he would be out of line to say something, but in the end, pushes forward. "Wyatt and I had talked about how you two weren't on speaking terms."

"I blame myself," Wyatt's father looks down and takes a

deep breath, "the worst part is that he wanted to get together right before he died. He even tried calling us up."

Nolan's eyes widen in surprise at the revelation that Wyatt had actually taken the plunge to get in touch with his father. He had originally thought that he'd be able to get Wyatt to make the first move after a few weeks of gentle prodding. Maybe months. But to hear that his talk with Wyatt had potentially helped these two bridge the gap even a little. Such an emotional avalanche was impossible to control. Nolan's eyes fill with tears. He openly began to weep.

"Oh my God, sir... Are you... Uh, are you okay?"

"I'm fine. I just... It's hard to hear that your son actually took what we talked about to heart."

Breaking through stifled sobs, "I guess he did. Did you know him well?"

"No... We only really talked recently. Oh! Where are my manners," Nolan wipes the tears off his face with a handkerchief and holds out his other hand, "my name's Nolan."

More out of muscle memory than anything, he puts out his hand and shakes while saying, "Henry, it's a pleasure. Well I mean..."

"I know what you mean. I felt the same way talking with your wife."

"Yeah. It's always difficult meeting new people at these kinds of events, especially when most common greetings give the wrong impression."

Both of them stand in silence for a bit while taking in the room. But soon Henry needed to ask, "So how long did you know my son?"

"We really only talked the one time. He was coming home late from a night out and we met in the hallway."

"Wyatt…was out? At night!?"

Stifling a laugh, "Oh yeah. He couldn't even get his keys in the lock. So I had him over for some coffee."

"That's amazing. He never seemed like the kind of person that would enjoy going out like that."

"He was happy. But it also seemed like him going out was something new. Something that he found out that he needed."

"I wish we could have talked more. There's so much left unsaid."

"Same here, we had made plans to get dinner. But that never happened."

Another silence comes between the two. But Henry felt pressured to ask, "You said that Wyatt talked about us?"

"Yeah. He didn't like how the relationship between you ended up, but he didn't know what to do about it."

"I wish we had been able to talk about what now feels like such a stupid and petty issue."

"Don't blame yourself."

"Why not? He's still dead, he didn't know how bad I felt over our rocky relationship, and now he never will."

"I talked with him the night before he died…One of the things we **DID** talk about was he didn't blame you. He thought that **you** were disappointed in him."

Henry took a deep breath. "He did so much for himself. He made his own company. He lived on his own. He seemed to enjoy what he did. He was my boy," with tears welling up in his eyes, Henry continues, "he was my everything. For his entire childhood, he was the reason I got up in the morning. He was the reason that I went to work, paid the bills, and went to the grocery store. If he was happy… If he was living the life he wanted… I could never be disappointed."

"They don't... They... can't understand what it's like. We know the pain of having to hold a child in your arms in a very specific way just to lull them to sleep. As well as the shooting pain holding them like that causes. And that you would gladly go through it to make sure they can sleep."

Henry lets out a miniscule laugh before saying, "the pain of sleeping on their bedroom floor because they're too sick and want you around so they can feel safe."

Nodding Nolan agrees, "we know... And they'll never really understand until they go through it themselves."

With sadness in his eyes, Henry asks, "So he really didn't blame me?"

"No."

"Thanks, it's nice of you to say."

"It may be nice, and it might be painful, but either way, it needed to be said."

They sit in a comfortable silence that grows between them. A knowledge of loss, grief, and understanding. Eventually, they continue to talk about less impactful topics before Henry leaves to talk with other mourners.

LINGERING NEED

Chapter 19

Sitting with hands covering his eyes to help hide the shame he feels, his vision tunnels. Understanding that what he thought of as a selfless gesture of sympathy has turned into a moment of personal distress and grief. A world full of people living their own lives, a city full of individuals, and it just so happens that he met both a father and son, and for that son to be fated to die.

Finally, Luke's turbulent emotions start to even out. Realization hits him. This is the second time he's been able to even out like this. Henry and his wife had gotten him to sit and calm down after the realization. After that, Henry was told to greet the other mourners that had shown up by his wife while she sat and rubbed Luke's back. She was understandably curious and asked a few questions about how Luke had known and met her son. At the end, she hugged Luke and thanked him for showing compassion to him.

This broke Luke.

He didn't know what to say. How to make her understand. How little he actually did.

He glanced up and could detect her understanding. She knew just how little was done. She also knew how much it meant in the moment. Knowing this, she understood that nothing else was possible. She knew Luke wasn't to blame.

But was he?

Blame is exactly what he feels. Blame for not staying with him longer. Blame for not making him better. Blame for not... not... nothing.

Luke knows logically that he couldn't have done anything. Hell, a taxi hit him. What amount of prayer the night before could have stopped a traffic accident? But as his heavy gaze got dragged down again, he heard a little voice saying, "guilt is guilt, and sorrow is sorrow."

Unfortunately, the thing that Luke has yet to realize and deal with is how bad he feels about not being sadder before he found out the ceremony was for Wyatt. He came here knowing that it was for someone who died. He knew that the father of that person was going through the most difficult thing a parent will ever need to go through. But at the end of the day, he felt nothing for the person who died. He felt bad for the father, but only because he wanted to help make him feel better. Luke wanted to grieve with Henry; he didn't want to take on that pain, or feel the loss himself. What Luke wanted was selfish. He did it all for himself, and he knows it. He just doesn't want to admit it.

Now he's alone. Luke looks up towards the ceiling and asks, "Why?"

Just one word, and he only asked it once. Despite that, it asked everything. It asked why God had taken the life of a man who had such a difficult time finding himself? Why was he taken after deciding to go to church? No. Wyatt didn't go for church. He went for God. Why was he taken after trying to find God?

"Why?" The word echoes inside Luke's skull.

Time passes, even though to Luke there was no time. He couldn't tell if it had been five minutes or five months. A great blankness had come over his mind while sitting in that chair. So, even though Luke was shocked to find someone sitting down in the chair beside him, he didn't react in the slightest.

"Name's Nolan."

The words reached him, but Luke couldn't respond. He had originally thought it was Henry again, but apparently not. For some ineffable reason, someone new has been injected into his life, again.

When will it end?

"I didn't know Wyatt all that well, but it... it always hurts when you know the person that dies."

Luke turns his head to look at Nolan, "the name's Luke," he lifts his hand out in greeting, "I didn't know him all that well either."

Nolan takes Luke's hand and they shake a somber hello. "How did you and Wyatt meet?"

Luke gathers his thoughts as Nolan gives him time. After what felt like too long, he replies, "We met at a church a few days ago. He was... We, were having a difficult time and sought comfort."

"I always found going to church to solve your problems only seemed to help when the problem being solved was finding a quiet place to think."

"It was really nice to know that someone else was having problems. Even if we didn't know each other, we could understand the importance of being there for each other, even if it just meant listening."

"Knowing that you're not alone in the world is a powerful feeling. Most men will go the majority of their life without a sympathetic ear that knows their pain. But the moments when someone you don't know, someone that doesn't even know your name is willing to stop everything and give you a helping hand... That's the feeling of a miracle."

Luke thinks about what Nolan said for a bit before replying, "My parents always said that I was never alone because God would always be there for me. They made it seem like God was someone that would pull up a chair after I had a hard day of work and talk about anything I wanted... But that's not true. It's never been like that."

"Belief that God is always there is helpful for many. But, when was the last time you had a problem that you shared with God and you felt like he was there to console you? When was the last time that God gave you a hug and made you a cup of tea?"

Those questions surprised Luke. He hadn't thought of it like that before and didn't know if he liked that line of thinking. "I don't really see how that matters. Especially when it comes to God and his love for me."

Nolan pauses for a few seconds and then says, "Okay. Imagine you had a friend that said they will always love you and they would always be there to listen. But when you do talk to them, you can't tell if they're even listening to you, and then when you're done talking they just sit there looking around without ever looking at you directly. How would that make you feel?"

Luke doesn't know what to say, but a look of grave understanding spreads across his face.

Nolan quickly interjects, "That is to say, a belief in God is not an inherently bad thing, and in most cases can be an extremely powerful and helpful way to deal with your problems.", a bit slyly he adds, "Just ask the citizens of Jericho after the wall fell. But... God can't replace human connection."

"Human connection?"

"Do you remember that feeling you had when, Wyatt was with you in church? When you felt the connection, that bond between two people where you could almost see each other's pain. That right there is what many people go searching for when they look to God."

Luke's eyes well up with tears and a lump forms in his

throat. It takes a few seconds, but he says, "Maybe I've been searching so hard and too long in the wrong places."

"No one can tell you that. Only you can say what is and isn't right for you as a person. You need to ask yourself why you go. Why you need God. And above all... You need to ask yourself if you believe."

"I went for my Mom... She loved it so much. I think she loved the community behind everything most of all. We would help out at every event on the calendar... She taught me to help without expecting anything in return. If someone was down on their luck, we would deliver a freshly made casserole along with a bag of canned food to take the strain off their budget. If someone's kids were in the hospital, we would go over to their house, we would clean and cook for the day so that they could spend time with their kid. She still does it... Every chance she gets."

"She sounds amazing."

"Oh, she is... But she taught me to believe. I found joy in church. I was able to find peace and tranquility praying to God. He gave me the strength to come to 'the big city' for this job, to leave everyone I knew, and to try and make it in the world."

Nolan smiled softly at Luke and said, "You've done so much for yourself. If you were my boy, I'd be proud. So why does it sound like you're having trouble?"

"That peace and tranquility that I got from praying... I don't feel it as much as I used to. It doesn't last as long, and it's been harder to find," Luke closes his eyes, puts his head in his hands, and with a tremor in his voice, he continues, "I think God might have forsaken me."

Shocked, Nolan takes a few seconds to fully comprehend what Luke has said and replies, "Luke. You seem like such a great kid. Hell, you're at the funeral of someone you only met once, and if I'm not mistaken, you originally didn't know who the funeral was for. You've done so much for so many. Have you ever asked for help yourself?"

"I… I guess not. It always felt like I was in a better place than those around me."

"There will always be someone that has it worse than you. If you go looking there will always be a man without a jacket, or a sick child that needs medicine. But you need to take care of your needs as well."

"But what would I need?"Luke shakes off the notion.

"How about love from those you care about? You could take some time off… Visit your hometown. You may just be homesick.I bet your Mom would love to help you relax and feel better."

As Luke thinks about Nolan's words more and more, the weight on his shoulders makes itself known. Thinking of taking some time off and going home means so much more than he realized. The pressure to always give had been wearing him down more than he had understood. His chest has trouble taking deep breaths. Luke feels a bit of water welling up in the corners of his eyes again, and he knew that what Nolan said was true. Too much was resting on his shoulders; he needed time to heal.

Luke remembers Nolan, patiently waiting next to him, so he looks over and says, "Thank you so much, it means a lot that you were willing to talk."

"It's no problem at all… It does seem like I've been doing that a lot recently. I just can't seem to help myself from butting into other people's lives and problems." Nolan says as he waves his hand dismissively.

A bit confused, Luke asks, "Why do you think that is?"

Nolan explains how he met Wyatt on Monday night and how happy he seemed to be. But after that, they talk about Wyatt's personal life. He became sad and in need of comfort. That's when Luke realizes they had both met Wyatt on the same day, only hours apart. Nolan explains how he tried to help Wyatt rekindle his relationship with his parents but that he hadn't expected anything to come of it in the short term. Going on to explain that after he found out that Wyatt had died, he seemed to keep going out of his way to find people in need of help.

"Isn't that a good thing?"

"Not if I'm just doing it to quell my own guilt."

"What guilt?"

It takes a bit, but Nolan finally responds, "I'm always the one to survive. It doesn't matter if they're friends, family, or even my wife. Every time one of them dies, I become a little lonelier. I become sadder and more isolated. I could go visit my children and their families, but then I'd be doing the same thing to them as what's been happening to me. Eventually I'm going to die. I don't want them to feel the kind of grief I've suffered."

"But doesn't that just lead to you suffering more."

Nolan refuses to answer. His face sets into grim determination as he realizes he has finally put into words the issue he's felt growing for years.

"You should interact so that both peoples' lives are better. You help those you can, you show people how to live a good life by example, and you pass on as much joy as you can to those that come after."

Luke can see the cracks in Nolan's facade as his words reach him.

Nolan reaches into his pocket and takes out a business card. He plays with it a bit as his face turns soft.

"Nolan? Are you okay?"

A bit more surprised than he should be, he answers in the affirmative and puts the card back in his pocket. Nolan thanks Luke for listening to his issues and giving a kind word. This makes Luke laugh a bit, and he says the same thing back to Nolan.

They sit together in silence for a bit as Wyatt's parents talk with the few other mourners that have attended. Both of them still mourn for the Wyatt they knew. It didn't matter how short of a time they knew him. But they also start planning for the moments after this room. For the things they will now do because they were in this room. They plan for the things that they will do because of Wyatt.

~SUNDAY~

A SAGE NUDGE

Chapter 20

"Why am I even here?"

Seth finds himself sitting at a bar, waiting for... **someone** to come and meet him. Yesterday he answered his phone to a cryptic question-and-answer session that ended in the man on the other end asking to meet him at this specific bar. So here he is, drinking alone because he was so anxious that he got here a half an hour early. Sipping on a gin and tonic hasn't helped his anxiety either.

Seth mumbles, "I understand you're looking for someone," under his breath.

He feels stupid for all the time he's spent over the last week pining over a girl that's refused to call him even once. Maybe he should just leave. She obviously doesn't want to see him. So why should he be trying this hard? It's because he actually liked her. Hell, he's tried to downplay his feelings more times than he could count after the first few days of no contact; but no matter what he did, he couldn't stop.

An older man walks up beside him and asks, "Are you Seth?"

Seth turns his head, looks the older man up and down and replies with a slow but deliberate, "Yes..."

Nodding his head a bit, the older man sits next to him. Leaving Seth more confused than anything, but a bit of anger flares as the old man flags down the bartender.

"Can you get me a double of my Scotch?" the man next to Seth places his hand back on the bar.

"Right away sir."

As the bartender goes to make the man's drink, Seth can't stand it anymore and just asks, "What are you her father?"

The old man smiles. Not a malicious smile, but the smile of someone who has felt pain and grief and is just trying to protect others from feeling the same thing. This broke Seth's composure. In that moment, he knew this man was here for his sake just as much as he was there for Dawn's.

"The name's Nolan, and for the purposes of this talk... Think of me as someone that cares about her more than her father does."

That hit Seth in the gut and a sullen expression crosses his face while he questions, "You're her lover?"

After a bit of laughter Nolan corrects, "No, but I am someone that understands a bit more of the situation than you."

The bartender returns with Nolan's glass and the two of them sit in a difficult silence while they each sip from their respective glass.

To break the ice, Nolan asks, "Do you drink Scotch?"

"I've been known to. But I'm not always a fan of the taste," he answers with a quizzical look on his face.

"You know, I started drinking Scotch when I was younger. At the time, I hated the taste with a passion."

"Let me guess, you wanted to act more manly by doing something you disliked."

"You're not entirely wrong. I just wanted to be the kind of man that drank Scotch..." Nolan's eyes look up as if remembering,

"I wanted to be the kind of man that sat in a high backed chair and could smoke a cigar and drink with his friends."

Seth's mind conjures images of his boss and his boss's boss. Both are the kind of men Nolan's talking about. In fact, Seth laughed a little when he realized that almost any man would know the type of person he was describing.

"You're still drinking Scotch, so you must have learned to like the taste." Seth lets out a derisive sigh.

"No... most of them still taste like ass." Nolan pauses to check for a reaction out of the corner of his eye before sipping.

It takes a few seconds for Nolan's words to kick in, but once they do, Seth chuckles. During this time, Nolan flags down the bartender.

"Pour him a single of mine." Seth notes Nolan's air of confidence.

"Will do," says the bartender as he walks away.

Seth stops laughing as the bartender returns with a bottle and glass. With a smile, he pours a shot into the glass and slides it in front of Seth. He nods his head and walks down the bar to put away the bottle. Seth and Nolan both share a glance.

"Try it." Nolan gestures.

Seth shrugs, picks up the glass, swirls the liquid, and takes a gentle sip while bracing for the harsh sting of alcohol. Eyes widen as he looks down at the glass of Scotch in his hand. Still surprised, he looks back at Nolan with a questioning face.

With a badly hidden smirk, Nolan presses, "A lot better than what you're used to?"

"H... How? I mean if they all tasted like this, I'd understand why someone would drink the stuff so much. But... How is **THIS** the same thing that I know as Scotch?" Seth stares at his swishing glass as if in disbelief.

"I learned a long time ago that if you want decent Scotch…" he takes a slow sip, "you'll have to be willing to pay a bit extra." Nolan's pride shines through.

"But that still doesn't explain how people can be, allowed, to let 'rail Scotch' and what's in this glass share the same moniker." Luke stares expectantly.

"It's an issue of time… They are technically the same thing. There are some differences when you start to get technical. But the majority of the issue is the age. Most people don't take the time to let it mature and change. Most people let their greed get the better of them and take the Scotch out early."

"So it's a money grab? They just want to turn a profit faster, so they put out an inferior product?"

"Something like that, there are other reasons. But I've always assumed most are just unwilling to wait for a good thing."

They both take a sip from their glass and enjoy themselves for a fleeting second.

Nolans' face becomes more serious. "So tell me what you see in her."

Seth thinks, puts down the glass, and responds, "She… Was so free. The way she talked about the world made me think of life in a new way… No… It was less than that," flush with embarrassment, he continues, "I felt as if she would make my life better just by having her there next to me… I don't know… It's all of those things, none of them, and so much more than I could ever put into words."

"Good." Nolan's eyes bore straight forward before turning to look at Seth.

"Good? What do you mean good?"

With sympathy softening his eyes, Nolan says, "Son… I was married to my highschool sweetheart. We loved each other until the day she died. What you just said is how I felt for her, from the day we met, 'til the day she died, and even now after all this time. The love I had for her isn't something I can easily explain or quantify... In the end, there's a part of myself that will never be whole again; because I'll never again have the gift of her presence."

After that, Nolan raises his glass and Seth responds by softly clinking their glasses together. They sip their drinks and sit in silence. Nolan knows Seth has to ask the next question.

"Why?... Why did you ask me here?"

"I wanted to know how you would react," Nolan says before taking a slow sip.

"What do you mean, how I would react?" Seth's voice rises an octave. "Maybe you mean how I would act when she doesn't talk to me for six days, with zero explanation, even though I'm positive we both had an amazing time. Or is it how I would react when after those six days some random man calls me out to a random bar to talk to me about her."

The bartender looks over at them with concern on his face. Nolan gestures that everything is fine. Meanwhile, Seth realizes how worked up he got and tries to calm down by cracking his neck, unsuccessfully, and then drinks a bit of Scotch to settle his nerves.

Nolan retorts, "Take a second for me... Think of how... she might feel if you learned something that would change the entire nature of your relationship... and in the end, you leave her."

"I wouldn't... There isn't..."

"There's always a way, and you know it... At some point, with enough weight, the chair you're sitting in will break."

"What could be so bad, that it would change how I felt that night?"

"The same thing that caused her father to disown her. The same thing that forced her out of her hometown and to move to the city."

Shocked and confused, Seth's head hangs down until it's almost touching his glass of Scotch. His mind races with thoughts of possible issues. But each time he comes back to asking himself, "What has she gone through?"

With a look of determination, Seth insists, "I don't care; I just want to be with her! The worst thing that could happen is if we didn't even try."

Nolan sips on his Scotch and smiles. As he puts down the glass, he notices the bar's door open. A lone person enters, and the door swings to close behind them. Nolan's smile widens a bit before letting Seth know, "I thought we would've had more time than this to talk..." Nolan can see the confusion on Seth's face as he continues, "The question is, when you take her home after a few drinks and you're both having a good time... Will you treat him like any other girl you bring back?"

Seth's confusion grows as Nolan gazes behind him towards the door. Nolan raises a hand to wave at someone and smiles widely.

Seth says, "Of course I wo... Wait, what?"

"Son... I've done my part," Nolan points over Seth's shoulder. "It's up to you two to figure out the rest."

Confused more than anything else, Seth looks over his shoulder. He sees a guy. Just a normal everyday guy walking closer while looking towards Nolan. But there's... something. Something familiar about his face. Something familiar about his walk. The man notices Seth and his face changes to shock. Fear and confusion war on the man's face. He stops dead in his tracks with a foot still partially lifted in the air. Seth's mind races to understand who he's looking at and why he seems so familiar. In that moment, everything clicks into place.

"Dawn?"

Seth's face changes from confusion to utter surprise and

looks back at Nolan for confirmation. Trying to say something, anything, but he can't seem to get the words to form correctly in his mouth. He looks back to see the man... Dawn, walking away fast.

"Wait!"

Seth gets out of his seat and hurries to pick up his things. He clumsily takes out his wallet to search for how to pay for the drinks. With a quick glance to Nolan, he half panic yells, "Thanks, or sorry, or, whatever, but I have to see a girl about a horse." Seth throws two hundred-dollar bills on the counter and rushes after Dawn.

Nolan's smile doesn't fade as he watches the figure of Seth disappear through the front door. He shifts back into a comfortable position, splitting his focus between the glass in his hand and the mirror behind the bar. Nolan takes the last sip of the almost empty glass.

"The rest is up to you two."

SECRET DREAD

Chapter 21

How! How was he there!

I need to go; I need to escape. Don doesn't flat-out run, he can't with the amount of people on the sidewalk, but he's fast. He's lived in the city for long enough that he knows how to be fast in a crowd. So that's what he does.

Why was he there? Why was he with Nolan? His mind racing nearly as fast as he is.

The sounds of the city are nothing compared to the thumping of blood in his ears. Each car driving by is just a haze of sound and a glimpse out of the corner of his eye. Even the people being passed on the street are only vague shapes of color.

Is he following me? No... He couldn't be. He wouldn't have had enough time. He wouldn't have wanted to. Not after seeing me... as me.

Seth had burst out the bar's door in a fright, trying to find out which direction she went but the crowds on the street made it almost impossible. But he could see someone faster than the rest, and that was all he needed. He chased after her.

Twenty feet.

"Dawn!"

Some people on the street turn to look or make quick questioning glances. This actually helps because there are those that move a bit out of the way, making it easier for Seth to catch up.

Don is still in a world of his own. He hears something loud behind him, but the pumping of blood is too loud.

Ten feet.

Seth's heart is jumping out of his chest. With every pump of his leg, he seems to close a bit of the distance.

Why here? Why now? It couldn't have been him. He wouldn't be following me!

Don slows for long enough to turn, and sees Seth. Not quite down at the end of the block, but close, too close. His eyes start to water and grow large with concern. He turns back. He wants to escape. He **needs** to escape. But how? His steps are getting slower, his body's not working like it should.

Five feet.

"Dawn… Please stop?"

The sincerity in his voice cuts through the rest of the world's noise. Don's legs start refusing to work properly, slowly veering off course until he stumbles into a wall.

Seth sees her stop hard against the wall of the building. Out of concern, he rushes forward, afraid that she might fall and hit her head. But as he closes the final distance, she appears to be stable. Her only movement is the jagged breaths and silent crying that seem to rack her body with every other breath. They stand there, both dreading the next step that is sure to come.

Finally, Seth moves. Raising his hand and extending it out. To reach out, not just through the physical distance that separates them, but through the vast chasm of pain, confusion, and regret. A soft touch to her shoulder sends a jolt of surprise through her body. Her entire body goes rigid.

Don feels a light pressure on his shoulder, soft and gentle with a warmth that he has craved even though he should know better. The thumping in his ears is gone, replaced by the sounds of cars and pedestrians walking past them.

Seth remembers this back. He fell in love with it on the dance floor, but now he sees it in the light of day, on the body of a man he's never met. Except he has. He recognizes the shape and feeling he gets from looking at her. He's terrified of going any further. He's afraid of finding out the truth, and for the truth to be more than he can handle.

Seth realizes he has to know. That he has to follow through and see this to the end. So he slowly grabs hold of her shoulder.

So softly that Seth almost doesn't hear it, "No…"

But he needs to know. He's wanted to see her for days now, and to be so close yet be unable to gaze upon her would hurt more than he could bear. But he can also see the anxiety and panic that just this touch has caused. So Seth wants Dawn to decide for herself.

"Please… I need to know." Seth's voice comes out raspy.

"Why?" Her voice laden with sorrow and restrained tears. "Why can't you leave that part of us separate?"

"I've wanted to see you again, no matter the cost."

"Oh really? Who is it you wanted to see?" Wiping back a few tears. "Do you want the girl that goes to clubs at night trying to build up her courage? How about the girl that spends most weekends with friends watching bad movies? Or the girl that spends her days working at a coffee shop hoping to get enough tips to get some better makeup?"

Seth stammers out, "I… I want."

"No!" In an almost crying yell that immediately softens, "You are going to listen."

There they stand, unmoving. Seth unyielding, willing to do anything that would help her in that moment.

Continuing after trying to swallow the lump in his throat, "Or do you want the person that was laughed out of high school for being too weird... The person that was forced to leave their hometown because even the police looked the other way when they were attacked!"

Seth's eyes widened in surprise. But he still refuses to talk, not until she's done.

After a bit, Don's voice becomes calmer. "Or is it the person that was beaten by their father because of the anger he felt for his son?"

As Don finishes, he turns around to look Seth straight in the eyes, tears streaming down his face in a cascade of emotion. Years of pent-up emotion finally bursting forth.

But Seth sees it all. He lets out a quick gasp as he takes in the person before him. Finally, having the time to truly process the person in front of him. Seeing a man, in all things. But in that same second, all he can see is the woman he's been looking for. Slowly, joy replaces the shock on his face.

Don has trouble understanding what he's seeing. Seth's eyes should burn with white-hot hate. Instead, they can see her for who she is.

Softly Seth lets her know, "I wanted you... It doesn't matter what happened in the past. I want to share my future with you."

Dawn's heart flutters in her chest, causing a new whirlwind of emotions that makes her eyes fill to the brim again. Any pain she felt seems to melt away as a new river of tears flows from her eyes. Dawn's knees give out a little and she almost falls to the ground before Seth catches her.

"I can't say that I've ever had a relationship like ours before, and if you had asked me a year ago if I thought that I would be fighting so hard for it, I would've probably laughed in your face. But, I… Feel this pull to you. Nothing is certain in life. You may find that I'm not the kind of man you want to be with. You might leave me tomorrow. But the worst thing either of us can do is go against our feelings and never try."

Sobbing into Seth's shirt, she heard every word, which made her cry even harder. After catching her breath, she looks up at Seth's face with small tears rolling down her cheeks. She lifts a hand slowly to her face to first wipe the lines of tears and then cup Seth's cheek.

"If you'll have me…"

And so,

in a rain of tears and hugs, they kiss.

Emotions flair and die,

pain is felt and lost,

trust is shaped and grown.

For in each other, they have found what most will not.

Together, they find love.